LOCKED DOWN HEART

COMBAT HEARTS SERIES #3

TARINA DEATON

Happy Reading!
Tarina Deaton

TARINA DEATON LLC

Photographer: Kruse Images and Photography

Cover Design: Imagination Uncovered

Editing: Jessica Snyder Edits

❀ Created with Vellum

For El.
You had me at, "What in the fresh hell is this s**t?"

ALSO BY TARINA DEATON

Stitched Up Heart

Rescued Heart

Half-Broke Heart

CHAPTER 1

oom. Boom. Boom.

Denise Reynolds rolled off the edge of the bed and took a defensive position. Heart pounding as she blinked sleep out of her eyes, she crouched in the small space between the bed and the wall and reached for her gun, groping in the dim light. Where the fuck was her gun?

A groan sounded from the bed and sheets rustled. The jangle of dog tags worked its way into her consciousness as she came fully awake. Sarah's house—not the desert. The dust ruffles on the bed should have given it away. Sprocket, her two-hundred-pound English Mastiff, eased herself off the bed and stuck her snout in Denise's face, bathing her with doggie breath and smearing slobber on her cheek.

"Ugh, quit that." She pushed her dog's huge head away and wiped her face with the sleeve of her worn t-shirt. "I'm awake." Sprocket huffed at her.

The pounding came again.

"Aunt Denny! Someone's at the door!" Her niece's high voice reached her from across the small house.

How long had she been asleep? Twisting her neck around to

look at the clock, the luminous numbers showed four-twenty-three. Seriously? She'd been out for less than fifteen minutes. Fifteen hard minutes if she woke up this disoriented. That hadn't happened since she started staying at Sarah's house a few months ago.

She'd sat on the end of the bed to kick her shoes off after coming home with the kids and told herself the universal lie of *I'll just close my eyes for a few seconds*. God, she was burning it at both ends between work, spending time with Sarah at the hospital, and taking care of Kimber and Kaden. She needed to figure out a better schedule.

Levering up out of the tight spot on the floor, she tried not to fall over Sprocket, who thought she was being helpful.

She reached between the mattress and the box spring for her Glock. Whoever was pounding on the door like that deserved to be greeted with the pew end of her gun.

"Come on." Pushing at the dog, she rose from her position on the floor and followed the dog out of the room.

"Aunt Denn—" Kimber stood in the door of the bedroom she shared with Kaden. Denise shifted her hand behind her back. "Someone's at the door."

"I heard. Sorry—I fell asleep."

"It's okay," Kimber said. "You've had a hard week."

Jeez, not something an eight-year-old needed to worry about. Denise needed to be better about being with them—they needed all the emotional support they could get right now. Her exhaustion would just have to wait. Or she'd have to start catnapping at her apartment during lunch.

"How's your homework going?"

She shrugged. "I'm done. I've been helping Kaden with his."

Why was she helping Kaden with his homework? He was a grade ahead of her. She made a mental note to ask Sarah about it when she visited next. "Okay. We'll sit down and go over yours after I see who's at the door."

2

Kimber put a hand on Sprocket. "Can Sprocket stay here?"

"Sure." Looking at the dog, she said, "Stay with K-Squared." Sprocket sat and licked her chops. "Good girl."

Holding the gun low beside her leg, finger poised along the trigger guard, she walked through the small, combined living room and dining room. She glanced through the peephole, then rocked back on her heels.

The bottom dropped out of her stomach then rushed up again to choke her. *What the fuck?* She stared at the door, trying to decide if she should open it or not.

Three more sharp knocks made the decision for her.

She unlocked the door and yanked it open.

"What the hell are you doing here?" she demanded.

Chris took a step back. Whether from the door opening suddenly, her, or her question, she wasn't sure. *He looks tired.* It wasn't her problem. Never was.

"Denise?"

"Yes, Chris. What are you doing here?"

The lines between his dark eyebrows grew more pronounced. "What are *you* doing here?"

His strong jaw was covered with stubble, accentuating the lines of his mouth. A mouth that was surprisingly soft, especially when it grazed over her skin. Her nipples pebbled under her thin t-shirt. Damn her traitorous body. It'd been almost seven months since he'd ghosted, it should have gotten the message by now and forgotten him.

"I asked first." She set her gun on the high shelf above the coat hooks and grabbed the zip-up hoodie hanging by the door, zipping it half way up.

"Why are you answering the door with a gun?" he asked.

"Because this isn't the greatest neighborhood and some asshole was pounding on my door." The neighborhood sucked. It wasn't the greatest when Sarah bought the small two-bedroom house and it had only gotten worse in the last five years. She was pretty sure her neighbor two doors down was dealing. As long as he wasn't cooking, and he kept it to his doorstep, she was willing to overlook it. But Kimber and Kaden were going to her parents the minute the school year was over.

"Why are you here?" She enunciated the question this time. She needed a quick answer so she could work on forgetting Christopher fucking Nolton. Again.

"I'm looking for Sarah Reed."

Her shoulders sagged, and she rubbed her hand over her eyes. "She's not here."

"When will she be back?"

She glanced over her shoulder. Sprocket sat in the opening of the short hall that led to the two small bedrooms at the back of the house. She let out a low woof and lay down, resting her head on her paws. She sensed Denise's stress, but was doing what she'd been told.

Denise stepped out of the house and pulled the door shut behind her, leaving it cracked. Chris moved back on the small concrete pad.

"She's not coming back. She's in the hospital with terminal cancer."

Light dawned in his eyes. "Shit. She's your cousin." Chris ran his hands over his hair. It had grown long and now curled around his ears and jawline. If it weren't for the stubble and dark circles under his eyes, he'd look boyishly charming. Things she should not be noticing.

She crossed her arms over her chest. "What is this about?"

He looked at the ground and took a deep breath before raising his head. "Her ex-husband was released from prison. He's skipped parole."

She dropped her arms. "What the fuck? He's not supposed to be out for another five years. At least."

His face pinched, like he had sucked on something sour. "He

4

made a good impression with the parole board. Got out early. I need to know why her ex has been calling her."

"What? He hasn't been calling her."

"Denise, he's been contacting her. We traced the calls to this residence."

Anger threatened to strangle her. "I guaran-damn-tee you, she hasn't had any contact with that fuckwad in almost ten years."

"Aunt Denny? What's going on?" Kaden stood in the now open doorway behind them.

She took a deep breath and schooled her features. "Hey, buddy. What are you doing?"

"I heard talking." He pointed at Chris accusingly. "Who's he?"

"Just a friend," she said. She brushed his hair back from his forehead. "Why don't you go back inside? I'll be there in a few minutes and we can read before dinner."

"Is Mom okay?" His voice broke at the end and his eyes became glassy.

"She's fine. We're still going to go see her Friday after school."

Kaden stared at Chris, eyeing him from top to bottom. He looked between them and asked, "Is this about the man that's been calling?"

She blinked and only by sheer will kept her voice even. "Why do you think this is about a man calling?"

Kaden looked back at Chris. "I heard him say someone was calling mom."

Denise glanced at Chris, trying to gauge his reaction. He stared intently at Kaden, but didn't ask any questions. "Has someone been calling for your mom?"

"Yes. He said he's our dad, but Mom said he was dead. He keeps asking where she is and when he can talk to her."

"What do you tell him when he asks that?" she asked.

"I tell him she can't come to the phone." He dropped his head and looked down at his toes. "Am I in trouble for talking to him?"

"Hey. No." She grasped his chin and turned his face toward

her. "You're not in trouble, buddy. I'll explain everything later, okay?" She kept her voice soft and steady. "I don't want you to worry about anything."

His gaze was too serious, too somber for a nine-year-old little boy. He shouldn't have a care in the world.

"Go back inside. I'll be in there in a minute." She kissed his forehead and turned him by his shoulders. "Go with Sprocket." She watched as he walked back into the house, hanging on to her dog's neck.

She leaned against the door jamb, facing Chris. "That answers your question."

"You need to warn him," he said, pointing through the open doorway.

She glanced over her shoulder to make sure Kaden wasn't in sight and spoke in a low voice. "I know. I don't know why Eddie's calling here all of a sudden. That fuckwit hasn't shown any interest in his kids since they were conceived. Why are you involved in this?"

He shoved his hands in the pocket of his jeans, pushing them a tad bit further down his lean hips. "I've been assigned to this case."

She blinked. "What case? Assigned how?"

"FBI, remember?"

"So?"

He looked off to the side and took another deep breath, letting it out through his nose. "I'm on a violent gang task force."

Understanding dawned. "Eddie was a member of the Southern Anarchists."

"Yeah."

She scrubbed her hands over her face. "I'll disconnect the phone tomorrow."

"We don't actually want you to do that."

She dropped her hands and stared at him. "I don't give a shit what you want. He's not having any contact with those kids."

"Denise, this is one of the few links we have to the Anarchists.

We need it. Just warn the kids not to give him any information when they talk to him."

Hard, dark memories threatened to push to the surface. "Let me say it again. I don't give a flying fuck. And you're sure as shit not using those kids as bait or as a way into a criminal gang. It's going to be a moot point in a few months anyway when I move them out of this house."

"Denise—"

"No. I'm not putting those kids in the middle of a war between the FBI and the Anarchists. I will do what I need to do to protect them. End of story."

She stepped back into the house and closed the door firmly. She wanted to slam it, but didn't want to upset the kids. How dare he? Who the hell did he think he was to show up after disappearing into thin air and ask her to use her cousins as a connection to a damn gang?

Jesus. She needed to talk to Sarah.

CHAPTER 2

The elevator dinged. Denise closed her eyes and took a deep breath, inhaling the astringent scent of disinfectant. She stepped out of the car and walked down the wide hall. Sprocket padded next to her, the black and red "service animal" vest snug around her chest. The hospital was one of the few places she wore it.

Stopping at the nurse's station, Denise leaned against the tall counter. "Morning, Nadia."

"Good morning, Denise. Hi, Sprocket." She smiled, flashing a deep dimple in her left cheek. "Can she have a biscuit?"

Jeez, had she ever been that young and innocent? "Sure."

Nadia popped the lid on the tin of dog treats the nurses had started keeping behind the desk when Denise became a regular visitor and held one out to Sprocket.

"Is she awake?"

Nadia glanced at the clock. "She was when I checked on her about half an hour ago, but she's been sleeping a lot lately."

Denise pulled her lips between her teeth and nodded. "How's she doing today?"

The nurse's smile faded and her eyes filled with sympathy. "I'll page the doctor and let her know you're here."

Denise looked at the desk and jerked her head in a semblance of a nod. "Thanks." She walked further down the hall to Sarah's room. Lifting the handle, she pushed open the door and entered the sunny private hospice room.

Her cousin reclined in the raised bed, her bald head pale against the pillows. The remote rested in her lax hand and her eyes were closed. Denise eased the remote away.

Sarah's fingers closed around it and her eyes popped open. "I'm watching that, Cousin It." Her voice was hoarse and broke in the middle.

"The TV's off, cue ball." She forced a smile.

Sarah looked at the small flat-screen mounted on the wall across from the bed. "It was on a minute ago."

"Uh huh." Denise sat in the large chair next to the bed and curled her legs under her bottom. Sprocket lay down next to her. A breakfast tray sat untouched beside the bed. "You didn't eat, pipsqueak."

"Don't call me that." Sarah pushed further up on the bed. "It's mush. Did you bring me a breakfast burrito?"

She scoffed. "After you blew chunks the last time? Hell, no."

A weak smile stretched the paper-thin skin across her cheeks. "Yeah. Probably a good idea. Wasn't nearly as good coming back up."

"Blech." Denise faked gagging.

"Oh, please. I've held your hair back plenty of times."

"True, but you don't have any hair."

"Touché." She closed her eyes. Denise worried she'd fallen asleep again, but her eyes fluttered open a few seconds later. "How're the kids?"

"They're good. I'll bring 'em by on Friday after school."

Sarah shook her head. "No."

Denise sighed. "Sarah."

"I don't want them to see me like this."

"I'm not going to let you distance yourself. They love you and miss you. Don't shut them out."

A tear spilled over her cheek. "I hate this," she whispered. "It's not how it's supposed to be."

Unfolding from the chair, she sat on the edge of the bed and held Sarah's frail hand between her palms. Sprocket raised her head, tuned into her emotions.

"They aren't going to have me for very much longer."

"I know, honey." Denise kept her voice soft. "But you need to let them have you for as long as they can."

More tears escaped as Sarah squeezed her eyes closed, but she nodded. "I just...I want their memories of me to be good ones. Not from when I was sick and dying."

"I'll make sure they remember all the good things about you. Mom and Dad will, too. You don't really think I'm going to hide all your horrible nineties high school fashion fails, do you?"

She smiled. "Those were all your hand-me-downs."

"Yeah, but they don't know that."

"Promise me you won't let them forget me."

She brushed her thumb across Sarah's cheek. "That'd be impossible. They're going to carry you around with them forever."

"Thank you," she whispered.

She kissed the back of Sarah's hand. Even though she felt like she'd said the right thing, how the hell was she supposed to comfort her? There were no words. No handbook. No how-to guide for the terminally ill. Her morbidity crept in and she selfishly couldn't help but hope that when it was her time it happened quickly instead of slowly dragging out over the course of months.

Now she had to dump more bad news on her cousin. "We need to talk about something else."

This was going to suck, but she needed to know. They'd never talked about what legal provisions Sarah had made for the kids. It was her fault. She kept thinking if she didn't talk about it, it wouldn't happen.

"Eddie was released from prison."

Sarah's eyes flew open. "What?" she gasped. "No. No!" She shook her head. "He's not supposed to be out for another five years. He can't be out."

"I know," she said softly, trying to calm her down. "I know."

Sarah sucked in air, hyperventilating. The machines beside her bed started beeping and Denise hit the call button. "Calm down, honey. Please."

Fear shone from her eyes. Sprocket stood and woofed as Nadia opened the door.

"What's—" Rushing to the bed, she lifted the oxygen mask hanging from the rack next to it. She fit it over Sarah's head and turned the valve on the wall.

Sarah inhaled deeply, never breaking eye contact with Denise. Her breath fogged up the clear plastic with each heavy exhale.

"What happened?" The nurse reached into the pocket of her scrubs and pulled out a stethoscope.

"I had to give her some bad news." Denise shoved her hands into her pockets and scrunched her shoulders.

Nadia held the earpieces over her ears. "Let's avoid doing that again, okay?"

Denise nodded. It was a lie. She had more.

Nadia listened to Sarah's chest, then removed the stethoscope and wrapped it around her neck. She grasped her tiny wrist and looked at her watch. After several seconds, she looked back at Sarah. "You okay now?"

Her breathing had evened out and her cousin nodded.

Nadia removed the mask from her face. "I'm going to hook you up to the nose hose." She opened her mouth, but the nurse cut her off. "I know you don't like it, but you need to wear it for a while."

She sighed. "Okay."

Nadia wrapped the clear plastic hose around each of her ears and adjusted the flow of air. She looked at Denise. "Not too much longer."

Denise nodded and waited for the click of the door closing.

Sarah's eyelids sank closed. "Tell me the rest." The blue circles under their depths seemed even more pronounced than they had only minutes ago.

Resuming her position on the bed, Denise wrapped her hands around her cousin's again. "He skipped parole."

The weak hand clenched. "How do you know?"

"The FBI came to the house looking for you."

She opened her eyes and tears spilled over. "How did they know where to find me?"

"Several ways, I'm sure, they're the FBI." Sarah didn't smile at her poor attempt at humor. "He's been calling the house." Denise licked her lips. "Kaden's talked to him a couple of times."

Sarah's hand crashed to her chest. "What?"

"Kaden has questions." She wasn't sure how much he and Kimber knew about the man who fathered them. "How much do you want me to tell them?"

Sarah took a shuddering breath. "All of it." Her whisper was harsh—full of pain, fear, and anger.

"Are you sure?"

Tears fell freely. "Yes. I wouldn't have chosen this, but they need to understand exactly how dangerous he is."

"Even what he did to you?" She didn't like that idea. Didn't understand the purpose of telling the kids.

"Use your best judgment. But tell them why he went to jail."

"Okay." Relief flooded through her. Thank God. She hoped she would never have to tell them exactly what kind of monster their father was. "We need to talk about their guardianship."

"I took care of it right after I was diagnosed." Her voice had grown weak and her lids drooped. The conversation had taken a lot out of her.

Guilt shimmied through Denise, but she needed to start making arrangements for the kids. "I'll talk to Mom and Dad about the best time to transition the kids. Might be best to wait for the summer since it's only a few months away." That way they wouldn't start a new school when the year was almost over.

Sarah fought to keep her eyes open. "You, Denise. You're their guardian."

"What?" Shock slammed into her, knocking the breath right out of her chest. "Sarah, that's not a good idea. Mom and Dad are the best option."

"You're the best option." Her voice was surprisingly strong.

"Sarah—"

"I love your mom and dad—more than my own parents—but they're too old to take care of an eight- and nine-year-old."

"I'm not equipped to take care of them. I don't know how to be a mom." Shit, some days she had a hard time taking care of herself. It'd never crossed her mind that her parents wouldn't get custody. They were making room in their house for K-Squared. That was the plan.

Sprocket put her nose in the back of Denise's knee and pushed. Her left hand fell to her dog's head.

"You've been doing it for the past three months."

"That's a temporary arrangement so they wouldn't have to move schools in the middle of the year," she argued.

Sarah's eyelids fell again. "Now it's permanent. I'm giving you the best of me." Her voice faded and she drifted off.

Denise palmed her forehead and stood. What was Sarah thinking? There were still periods she struggled to make it through the day. How was she supposed to do that with two kids?

Sprocket all but sat on her feet and stared up at her. "Rawr rawr." She sounded like Scooby-Doo.

Her wet nose pushed at Denise's hand and she scratched her behind the ear. "I'm not freaking out girl, but...fuck."

A soft knock sounded before the door opened and Sarah's doctor peeked her head in.

Denise moved to the door and stepped out of the room, holding the door for her dog. "Morning, Dr. King. She just fell asleep."

"Good. She needs to rest." She slipped her hands into the pockets of her white coat.

Do they learn that stance in med school?

"Nadia said she had a small episode."

Guilt played at the edges of her mind. What a cluster. "Yeah. I had to give her some bad news." Dr. King gave her a stern look. "It was something she needed to know, Doc. I wouldn't have told her otherwise."

"It's important that she not become agitated."

She stared over the doctor's head, down the long hall. It wasn't going to be much longer. That's what she was hinting at. *Wow, she's short.* The errant thought popped into her head. She needed to focus. And not on how she felt like a giant standing next to the petite doctor. "How long?"

Dr. King pressed her lips together. "Weeks, but that's honestly optimistic. More likely *a* week."

Denise took a shuddering breath. *Fuck.*

CHAPTER 3

*D*enise pushed open the door and ushered the kids in under her arm. "Shoes off."

"Can we play with the dogs in the back?" Kimber's big, doe-brown eyes stared up from her porcelain-doll face. One of her pigtails had drooped, giving her a lopsided appearance.

"Please, Aunt Denny?" Kaden, a male version of his sister, chimed in.

"Go ask Aunt Bree."

"Yay!" They bounded out of the mudroom and into the kitchen, yelling for Bree. Denise knew she'd let them play outside. Hell, they deserved it after the morning they'd had.

She sighed and kicked off her shoes. Sprocket sat and licked her chops, staring up at her. "Go on. You can play, too." Giving Denise a big puppy grin, she trotted after the kids. Sometimes she wondered if Sprocket forgot she was a dog. Or maybe she was the one who forgot Sprocket was a dog.

"Hey. How'd it go?" Bree stood at the counter chopping vegetables.

Denise opened the fridge and pushed food around the make room for the bowl of fruit salad she'd brought. "As well as can be expected." She grabbed the pitcher of tea Bree always had ready. "Sarah slept a lot and the kids were sad."

Setting the pitcher down, she stared at the counter. "Am I doing the right thing? Making them see her when she's like this?"

Bree stopped chopping. "They'll regret the time they missed later in life if you don't."

Leaning back against the counter, she ran her hands over her face, before scraping her hair behind her ears. "Maybe. What if I'm just damaging them?"

"Kids are resilient." Her friend leaned a hip against the counter. "Have you talked to Dr. Tailor about it?"

"Yeah." She dropped her hands. "She gave me a reference for a grief and family counselor, but I can't get an appointment till next month."

"Your parents going to take them?"

It welled up out of nowhere, an unstoppable force she had no control over. She dropped her head and blew out a breath, letting her hair fall around her face like a curtain.

"What?"

Fighting to keep her emotions at bay, she struggled to speak past the lump in her throat, but all she could do was shake her head. God, she hated this stupid fucking weakness.

Bree crouched down to look at her through the curtain of hair. "Denise...what?"

A tear escaped. "Sarah's giving me custody." Her voice sounded harsh in her own ears.

A second tear followed the first then a third.

"Shit." Bree grabbed her hand and pulled her out of the kitchen, down the hall to her bedroom. Closing the door hard, she thumbed the lock. "Talk."

"What am I going to do?" Tears flowed freely, no matter what she did to stop them. Why couldn't she stop them? She sat on the bed, defeat hammering at her defenses.

Bree sat next to her and pulled Denise's hand into her lap. "About what?"

"Everything. I don't know how to take care of kids."

"You can't do any worse than some people," she said dryly.

She pulled her hand away. "Bree, I'm being serious."

"So am I." She reached over and snagged some tissues from the box by the bed. Handing them to her, she waited while Denise blew her nose. "Lay it out. What's your first concern?"

She wadded up the tissue and tossed it on the bed next to her. "That I'm going to screw up. That I'm going to screw *them* up."

"Do you love them?"

"Of course I do."

"Then I'm pretty sure you can't screw them up. Next?"

She sighed and tilted her head back, unsure whether Bree's dismissiveness was helpful or not. "Where are we going to live? We can't live at the rescue in my little apartment and I refuse to stay at Sarah's. The area isn't safe and the schools suck. And that's another thing." She threw up a hand. "How do I even begin researching schools?"

"Well, the schools in this district are good."

"Okay. But I can't afford a house in this area."

Bree bit her lip. "You could if you rented my house."

Her brows pinched together. "What?"

"I was going to tell you this afternoon while we were getting the food ready, but Jase and I are moving in together. To his house."

"Oh my God! When did that happen?"

"The day after Gran's birthday."

"You mean the day after you freaked out?"

Bree rolled her eyes. "Yes, the day after I freaked out."

Denise hugged her. "I'm so happy for you."

"Thanks." Bree squeezed back, then released her. "But that means I need to get a renter." She shrugged. "I'd rather rent to you than to some stranger."

She leaned back. "I can't afford the rent on this house."

Bree gave her a baleful look.

"Bree."

"Denise."

She knew that look. Sometimes the woman could be even more stubborn than she was. "You're not going to let this go, are you?"

"No. The house is perfect for you and the kids. And it saves me having to hire a management company because I know you'll take care of it."

Sucking up her pride, she gave Bree a small smile. "Thank you."

"You're welcome. All that was superficial. You'd have figured it out on your own given enough time." She tilted her head, her gaze searching. "Tell me why you're really scared." Her voice was low. She was going to force Denise to say it.

To give voice to her greatest fear.

"What if...?" She swallowed and shifted her gaze away. "There's still a lot of darkness inside me. I still have nightmares where I'm interrogating someone."

"Okay?"

"It scares me. That I still have them. That, somewhere inside me, that person still exists. That I'm still capable of doing those things."

Bree leaned forward. "You are a long, long way from that ever happening again, Denise."

"Am I though? What does it say about me that I could even do that to another human being? I'm not a good person."

"When was the last time you talked to Doc Tailor?"

She blinked. "A couple weeks ago. Why?"

"Because you are so far off the mark about who you are, it's not even funny. You save puppies, for crying out loud. It's not like you're trolling bars for unsuspecting guys to torture in your basement of horrors. It was your job and you did it. It doesn't define who you are as a person."

"But I was really good at it," Denise said. Really, really good at it.

"So? I'm good at my job."

"You help people."

"So did you. Maybe not in the conventional way, but how many lives were saved from the intel you got from detainees?"

"It's not the same," she said, shaking her head.

Bree pursed her lips in frustration. "I think you need to talk to Doc Tailor about these particular ideas you have, but why exactly do you think it will affect K-Squared?"

"What if they try to wake me up during a nightmare? What if I hurt them somehow? Lose my temper because I'm having a bad day? What if I start to have *those* thoughts again?"

"You mean hurting yourself?"

"Yes."

"It's been years, Denise, why do you think it would happen now?"

Because it was always in her, playing in the far corners of her mind. That one moment when it seemed like it would be so easy to make everything stop. It was never an active thought—more like a bad memory that lingered. Shame that, no matter how hard she tried and no matter how much therapy she had, would never go away. It would always be there to remind her that at her weakest, she'd almost given up.

"I still have dark moments. Never as bad as it was then, but still. They don't need to see me like that. Not after watching their mom get sick. How can I be there for them, when there are times I have a hard time being there for myself?"

The door rattled, followed by a knock.

"Hang on." Bree squeezed her leg and answered the door, opening it a crack.

"Everything okay?" Jase asked.

"Yeah. We just need a few minutes."

"Okay. Chris's here."

"Oh," Bree said. That word contained a wealth of questions she knew Bree would ask. "Okay. We'll be out in a bit."

Denise dropped back on the bed and stared at the ceiling, errant tears sliding down her temples into her hair. She heard them kiss and indistinct whispering before the door clicked closed.

A dull pain echoed in the hollowness of her heart.

Bree sat on the bed, one leg bent, and looked down at her. "I'm going to let you in on a secret."

This should be good. Bree had become very philosophical since almost being killed by her deranged assistant. "What's that?"

"When you care about someone more than yourself it makes you stronger. More resilient."

Not likely. Denise turned her head. "I think that ship has sailed."

"I was talking about the kids. Who were you thinking of?"

She stared back at the ceiling. "No one in particular."

"Then what ship were you talking about?" Nope. She wasn't going to let it go. "The S.S. Christopher Nolton, by chance?"

That deserved a glare. "You just kissed Jase. Who else was I supposed to think you meant?"

The stupid woman grinned at her, having no idea how close she was to having her head shaved while she slept.

"Your death glare doesn't work on me." Her smile faded and her eyes lost their teasing light. "Kimber and Kaden. You love them. You will do anything to protect them and keep them safe."

A heavy weight settled in her chest. "What if what I need to protect them from is me?"

"You'd never hurt them." Her voice was strong, sure. Bree's belief swept over her. "If I thought that for even a second, I'd be the first one to support your parents taking them." Absolute trust.

"Not physically. But emotionally? What do I do if—"

"You call me. You call your parents. You call Gran." Bree stood and jammed her hands on her hips. "Why the hell are you acting like you're going to be doing this by yourself."

She came up on her elbows. "Because I'm worried I'm going to screw them up and they're going to hate me."

"Tell you what. How about if I promise to tell you when you're being a raging, selfish cow? Like now."

That brought her back up to sitting. "How the hell am I being selfish? I'm trying to do what's best for K-Squared."

"Have you asked them what they want?" Her voice rose and she pointed toward the rest of the house. "How do you think they're going to feel when they lose their mom and then their aunt because you pawn them off on your parents?"

Fuck. She flopped back on the bed. She was being selfish. "I hate you. You know that, right?" There was no heat in her words.

"You love me." The bed moved as Bree sat back next to her. "You hate when I'm right."

"Whatever." She blew out a breath. "There's more."

"Afraid they're going to find your vibrator collection?"

Her head popped up, eyes wide. "Holy shit. I didn't even think about that. Where am I supposed to hide them?"

Bree chuckled. "Between your mattress and box spring."

"I can't put them there—that's where I keep my gun at night."

"Top of your closet then."

"See! I'm not prepared for this. But that isn't it." She jackknifed up and twisted her hair behind her neck. "Eddie's out of jail. He jumped parole."

"Fuck. Does Sarah know?"

"Yeah. I told her Tuesday."

"Your parents?"

She shook her head. "Not yet. I'm going to tell them today."

"How'd you find out?"

Here come the questions. Taking a deep breath, she said, "Chris told me. He came looking for Sarah."

Bree pursed her lips. Jeez, she could see her wheels turning.

"How'd that go?"

"Well, I didn't shoot him, so I'd say it went okay."

Her lips twitched. "Why was he looking for Sarah?"

"He's involved in the investigation into the gang Eddie belongs to."

"When did that happen?"

"Eddie or Chris?"

"Chris."

"Monday."

"Hmm."

No bombardment? No twenty questions? "That's it? 'Hmm?'"

Bree stood. "Oh, I've got more. I'm just going to wait and see how today goes."

Rolling her eyes, she pushed up from the bed. "Today will be fine. We can all be grown adults."

Bree paused with her hand on the doorknob. "One piece of advice? If you don't want to get caught, don't run. I have a feeling he likes the chase." She winked and breezed out the door.

What the hell does that mean?

CHAPTER 4

*D*esire punched Chris in the gut. Somehow or another, Denise had only become more beautiful since the last time he'd seen her. He'd thought it the other day when he found her instead of her cousin. Jesus, that had thrown him for a damn loop. He tried to remember if she'd ever mentioned her cousin's name, but he didn't think she had.

She twisted her thick, honey-blond hair up into a knot on top of her head and wrapped a rubber band around it. Standing with her hands on her hips she looked down at the little boy he knew was her cousin. Second cousin? Although both he and the little girl called her "Aunt," so who knew. He had wondered for a second if she'd kept having kids from him when they were together. They were both mini versions of her. Same hair and eye color. He made a mental note to dig up a picture of Sarah Reed to see how similar she and Denise looked.

He pushed his hair away from his forehead. It'd gotten longer than he liked to keep it while he'd been undercover. Though on the list of shit he'd had to concede, it was pretty damn low.

Leaving Denise with no warning at all topped the list. She was holding a grudge, not that he could blame her. Trying to pass her a message at the last minute hadn't been ideal, but she of all people should understand sometimes the job took more than you expected. Her indifference to his return bugged the crap out of him. Running into her at her cousin's hadn't been the plan. The plan had been to call her and then take her out to dinner, explain everything to her—what had gone down and why he'd been called in so suddenly. Apologize and make it right, hopefully pick back up where they'd left it. Or at least close to where they'd left it.

Jase approached him with a beer in each hand and held one out to him. "You good, man?"

Chris took the beer and raised it in a silent toast. "As good as can be expected." Which was pretty damn bad, all things considered. He downed a good portion of the bottle.

"What's up with your leg?" Jase pointed with the bottom of his beer.

Chris looked down and sighed. "Took a knife to the thigh." More like a hatchet.

"Shit. What the hell happened?"

Chris swallowed a sip of beer. "I'll tell you when the drinks are stronger and the ears aren't so small." He nodded his head toward Kaden, who stood with his hand on one of the dogs, staring at them.

Jase looked between Kaden and Chris. "Why does he look like you're going to steal his dog?"

"I didn't get the warmest reception from Denise when I showed up at their house the other day looking for his mom."

"Sarah?" Jase asked. "She's in hospice."

The little girl, Kimber, called Kaden's name and he walked away from them.

"Yeah. We didn't have that intel," Chris said.

"Intel? Ah, fuck. Is this about her ex?"

Chris's focus honed in on his friend. "You know about him?"

Jase shook his head. "Just enough to know it's a good thing he's in jail."

"He's out."

"Shit. Does Denise know?"

"I dropped that bombshell on her when I found her instead of Sarah Reed."

His eyebrows rose and he looked like he was pondering something in his head. "Was that the first time she'd seen you since you've been back?"

"Uh, yup." He swallowed the last of his beer.

"That's a pretty compact shovel you've got there. Can hardly see it."

"What shovel?"

"The one you're using to dig that huge fucking hole you're in."

Chris rolled his eyes, but Jase wasn't wrong. He was living Murphy's Law. If it could go wrong, then it would. His hair fell into his face and he tried to tuck it behind his ears. He growled in frustration when it wouldn't stay put. What he needed was some clippers, but of course his had quit working. And his beer was empty.

Fuck you, Murphy.

"Jase!" Bree yelled from the kitchen.

"Yeah, babe?" he asked over his shoulder.

"You gonna cook this meat or what? The natives are restless."

"Coming." He turned back to Chris. "The woman wants my meat."

"Dude. How long you been saving that for?"

Jase laughed. "A while. Bree doesn't appreciate my humor nearly as much as she should."

He couldn't imagine why. "Do tell."

"I think it's because she compares mine to Denise's. That woman is the queen of one-liners." He jerked his head toward the kitchen. "Come on. You can help man the grill."

He nodded and followed him through the kitchen to the back deck, grabbing another beer along the way. He leaned against the railing and scanned the large yard. The kids ran back and forth with Bree's dogs, while Denise's dog lay in the shade of a large magnolia.

"This is a nice property," he said.

"You didn't see it last time you were here?"

"We didn't come out back, just stayed in the kitchen."

"Oh, yeah. It was Bree's grandparents.'" He threw burgers on the grill and dropped the lid. "We talked about moving in here, but decided my place made more sense since I use the back of the property for V.E.T. Adventures."

Shifting his hips against the railing to take some of the weight off his leg, he teased out the information Jase didn't come right out and say. "You're moving in together?"

A huge, shit-eating grin spread across his face. "Yeah."

Chris sipped his beer. "It looks good on you."

"What's that?"

"Domestic bliss." It did. His friend no longer had that hollow, haunted look that had been a constant since his best friend Tony's death.

"Damn straight." He lifted the grill lid and flipped the burgers. "You should try it."

He shook his head. "Pretty sure I've lost any chance of that."

"Doesn't hurt to give it another shot. Second chances do happen."

Bree stepped onto the deck with two bowls of food before he could respond. She set them on the table, then joined them at the grill and slid an arm around Jase's waist.

"How much longer?"

He slung an arm around her shoulders and kissed her. "'Bout five minutes."

Chris shifted his gaze away from them and locked eyes with Denise as she exited the house. Her eyes flared and then went flat before she looked away and set down the plates she was carrying.

That hollow feeling he'd had since leaving months ago spread a few inches deeper in his chest.

She put two fingers in her mouth and blew a sharp whistle. "Kimber! Kaden! Come wash up."

The kids ran up the steps, across the porch, and into the house, their shrieks of laughter and two dogs following them.

"See," Bree said to Denise. "Perfect."

"You don't have to sell it to me. I already said yes."

"Yes to what?" Jase asked.

"Denise is going to move into the house with the kids. It's perfect. There's plenty of room and the schools in the district are some of the best in the state."

"I said yes, Bree. Quit Vanna Whiting your house."

Bree dropped her arm from around Jase. "Did you just use *Vanna White* as a verb?"

"I don't know any of the models' names from *The Price is Right* or I would have used one of them as a verb instead."

Chris looked down at his shoes to hide his grin. God, those two were a riot when they were together. He'd forgotten how funny they were while he was knee-deep in the excrement of human existence during the last assignment. Denise's sarcastic wit was one of the things that had attracted her to him in the first place.

The kids burst out of the house. "All clean, Aunt Denny."

"Good job. Can you guys get cups and the pitcher of water and bring them out?"

"Okay," the little girl said. They ran back into the house.

"Do they ever walk anywhere?" Bree asked.

"Not usually."

The kids returned with the cups and pitcher and everyone jockeyed for seats around the table. For one awkward moment, he thought he and Denise would end up sitting next to each other, but Kimber asked Bree to sit by her, leaving him the seat at the end of the table.

Disappointment and relief warred for top billing position. He wanted a chance to talk to her, but here and now would be uncomfortable. Better to try to get her alone after dinner.

A lock of hair fell across his eyes when he reached for the coleslaw. Shoving it behind his ears wasn't working. "Bree, do you have any hair thingies?"

"Pretty sure she's got some bows and ribbons you can use, Rapunzel," Jase said.

Kimber giggled next to him and he winked at her.

"Don't be an ass." Bree whacked Jase in the chest with the back of her hand. "I have some hair ties. I'll grab you one."

"Why don't you just buzz it?" Jared asked around a mouthful of burger.

"You got clippers?"

"Yeah."

"No!" Kimber wasn't giggling. "If you cut your hair, you'll lose your magical powers."

"This is your influence." Denise glared across the table at Bree. She wore an amused smile. "I take all the credit."

"You can't cut it!" Tears welled up in the little girl's eyes.

"Kimber, sweetie, it's just hair. It will grow back," Denise said, reaching for the girl's hand.

She snatched her hand away. "It won't! All of Mommy's hair fell out and she's going to die!" She shoved back from the table and ran into the house. Denise's dog quickly rose from where she lay and trotted after her. It was the first time he'd seen the dog do anything other than mosey.

He swallowed hard, at a total loss for how to handle this kind of situation. Murderous gang? Sure, no problem. Hostage stand-off? Bring it on. Little girl faced with the reality that happy endings are few and far between? Complete and utter blank.

On his left, Kaden sat quietly with big fat tears rolling down his pale cheeks.

Denise scooted back her chair and reached for him. "Come on, buddy. Let's go talk to your sister." She hefted the little boy in her arms, no easy feat since he was almost as tall as she was. His thin arms and legs wrapped around Denise and he held on as if she were his lifeline. And she was. She was almost all those two kids had left in the world.

And their father was a wanted criminal he'd been charged to find and arrest.

Fuck. Murphy was an asshole.

CHAPTER 5

*C*hris pushed at the food on his plate. Should they check on them? What was the protocol in this kind of situation? He should have just gone to the barber when he realized his clippers were busted.

Jase leaned over and kissed Bree on the temple. "They'll be alright, babe. We'll make sure. Okay?"

She nodded roughly then swiped a tear from her cheek and took a deep breath. "Right. I have an idea." She looked at Chris. "Come with me."

Pushing back from the table, he and Jase followed Bree into the house, down the back hall, to what he assumed was the guest bedroom. Denise lay on the bed, Kaden and Kimber sandwiched between her and Sprocket. Kimber had her arm thrown around the large dog, her face buried in its neck. Kaden hugged his sister's back while Denise hugged them both. Her voice was low and he couldn't make out what she was saying.

Bree somehow squeezed herself onto the sliver of space on the bed behind Denise and rested her chin on her friend's shoulder, reaching over her and Kaden to rub Kimber's back.

"Sweetie, I have a plan. Do you want to hear it?"

Kaden lifted his head. "I want to hear it."

Denise rubbed his arm and he laid his head back down.

"If you and Kaden cut Chris's hair, he'll be able to keep his special powers," Bree said.

He straightened from the doorway. Whoa. What? He looked at Jase, whose shoulders shook with mirth.

Jackass, he mouthed.

Jase flipped him the bird and kept laughing.

"How do you know?" Kimber's voice was small, a slight hitch in her breath from crying.

"I looked it up in the secret Disney princess handbook."

Kimber's head whipped around as far as it could. "That's not a real thing."

Bree sucked in an outraged breath. "It is, too! I can't show it to you until you're older, though. You have to be twelve."

"I'm only eight." She dropped her head back on to the bed.

The initial crisis must have been resolved because Bree unwrapped herself from the group and stood. "I know, but I'll share the secrets I can."

"Promise?"

"Cross my heart."

"You guys ready to cut Chris's hair?" Denise asked.

"Yes!" Kaden broke free of his aunt's hold and scooted off the bed.

"I guess." Kimber didn't seem as enthusiastic about the prospect.

Right there with ya, little girl.

Denise moved closer to her and wrapped her arms around her, kissing the back of her head.

Kaden stood in front of him, starring up expectantly. "Can I shave patterns in your head?"

"Uh. Sure. I guess."

"Cool."

How did he get roped into this again?

Bree stopped next to him. "You ready for this?"

"Do I have a choice?"

"No. Not really." She patted his chest. "Consider it your civic duty."

"Hey," Jase said, grabbing Bree's wrist. "Hands to yourself, Grabby McGrabberson."

"It was a conciliatory gesture," she said.

"You were feeling him up."

She shrugged. "Tomato, toh-mah-toe."

"Yeah, I'll show you toh-mah-toe later."

Chris shook his head. "Hello, I'm standing right here."

"Good point. Jase, go get your clippers. We have a head to shave."

He watched her march down the hall, a woman on a mission. "She seems a little too excited about this."

"She gets like this sometimes. Usually we shoot some targets and she works it out of her system." Jase shrugged and traced Bree's path.

Great. Shaving his head was the alternative to his buddy's woman shooting things.

When he glanced back in the room, Kimber had rolled over and was hugging Denise. She twirled one of the little girl's pigtails around her finger while they lay there.

She glanced up and caught him staring. "We'll be out in a few minutes."

The first time she spoke to him all day was to dismiss him. Not that he blamed her. This was a family moment and he wasn't family.

The thought caused his heart to stop for a nanosecond and restart with a hard thud. How did things get so damn screwed up? And how did being part of a family, of Denise's family, suddenly become the most appealing thing in the world?

When he arrived on the back deck, Jase had his clippers

plugged into an extension cord and was showing Kaden the different attachments for length.

"Can we start now?" he asked.

"Let's wait until Kimber's ready. I think she should get the first turn. I'm sure there's a princess rule about it in Bree's secret book," Chris said.

His shoulders drooped. "Okay."

Crap. Now he'd made Kaden sad. Maybe there was a kitten around he could kick. "But I'll tell you what. We'll use one of the longer cutting lengths so you have enough hair to cut patterns in. How about that?"

Kaden's little legs kicked out and he bounced in the seat. "Okay."

Denise and Kimber arrived holding hands and joined them around the table. Jase found a stool for the kids to stand on so they could reach the top of his head. Bree wrapped an old towel around his neck and shoulders. He couldn't see her, but Denise's presence was as heavy as a physical touch at his back.

He flinched at the sharp pop when the clippers turned on and closed his eyes when Kimber took the first pass.

The feather-light brush of falling hair touched his cheek and Kimber giggled behind him.

"Can I do another one?" she asked.

"Go for it," Jase said. "Just leave some for your brother."

It was only hair. Right?

HE LEANED CLOSER to the mirror and rubbed his hand over his head, trying to figure out where the patches of hair remained. The kids hadn't done a completely horrible job, but he looked like he'd lost a fight with a weed eater wielded by a monkey on a three-day bender. Thankfully, Jase hadn't let them take the length attachment off so he still had some fuzz to work with and wouldn't have to shave his head completely bald.

Someone knocked on the bathroom door. "Come in."

He stood upright when Denise walked in and closed the door behind her. Her expression was unreadable. Not that he'd ever been able to read her anyway. She didn't emote the way other people did. If she didn't want someone to know what she was thinking, they never would.

"You missed a few spots in the back," she said softly.

"I'm having a hard time seeing back there without another mirror."

She nodded and stepped away from the door, holding her hand out for the clippers. He handed them over without a word and watched her in the mirror.

At least she was touching him. Even if it was only to push his head forward. He could feel her heat at his back. The slight brush and weight of her breasts when she moved her arms to reach the top of his head.

This was hell.

"Thank you for letting them do that," she said.

He swallowed hard, fighting the urge to turn around and kiss her. "You're welcome."

"They haven't had a lot to smile about in a while."

"Denise—"

"But it doesn't change anything. They aren't bait. They aren't a tool for you to get to your target. They're two little kids whose world is crashing down around them."

"I would never use them as bait, Denise."

She shut off the clippers and set them on the counter, finally meeting his gaze in the mirror.

She turned to leave the bathroom and he laid his hand on the door. "I was going to apologize. Show up at your apartment with flowers and chocolate and explain what happened."

"What happened with what?" She crossed her arms and shook her hair over her shoulder.

There. He saw that—the hurt and anger that she locked down before they could reach the surface.

"I left a note for Phil, my partner, to give to you but he never got it. The team that picked me up cleaned out my truck before they parked it at headquarters and they threw it away. I didn't find out until after I went to your cousin's house. That was the first full day I was back." He reached for the strand of hair over her shoulder, but she moved back. He dropped his hand. "I never meant to take off without telling you I was leaving."

"I get it, Chris. It's part of your job. Thank you for explaining." She reached for the doorknob.

"Denise, please."

"Please what, Chris? Please understand? I understand, I do. But it doesn't change anything. We hooked up." She shrugged her shoulders. "It was fun. But that was then, and my priorities have changed."

She took a deep breath. "Sarah is giving me custody of Kimber and Kaden. They're my priority now." She gestured toward the door. "So I can't afford to be someone else's afterthought."

She pulled the door open and walked away.

He eased it closed and rested his head against the wall next to it, holding on to the knob with a death grip to keep from punching the wall. Damn it. He wanted to chase after her, but he knew it would only make her angrier.

She'd never been an afterthought. She was pretty much his only thought.

CHAPTER 6

"*W*hy do you have to walk us to the bus stop, Aunt Denny?" Kaden asked.

"Because I want to make sure you don't run off and join the circus."

"That's silly," Kimber said. "Who would run off to join the circus?"

Denise flipped the end of Kimber's ponytail. "I wanted to join the circus when I was your age."

Kimber screwed up her face. "Why?"

"I wanted to be a lion tamer."

"That would be cool," Kaden said. "Did you know there are safaris in Africa where you can pet lions?"

"There are?"

"Yeah. And see whole herds of elephants."

"That would be really cool. I'll have to look into that. Maybe one year for your birthday." She had no idea how she would swing that. Maybe she could talk her parents into helping out with the cost of airfare and make it a combined birthday-Christmas gift.

They reached the top of the street where a small gaggle of kids stood, waiting for the early morning school bus.

"See, Aunt Denny," Kaden said, going back to sullen. "No one else's parents are waiting with them."

Stopping, she leaned down so her face was level with Kaden's. "Do you want to know a secret?"

He looked skeptical, but nodded his head. "There are no other parents here because they don't really like their kids."

His little jaw grew slack and he gaped at her for a few seconds before snapping it shut and scowling at her. "That's not true."

She nodded solemnly. "It is. Their parents probably say they can't because they have to work, but that's the real reason they aren't here."

"You have to work," he accused.

"I do." She shrugged. "I guess I like you too darn much to care. But you're not allowed to say anything. It would hurt the other kids' feelings if they knew the truth."

The school bus arrived and stopped at the corner. "Don't forget I'm going to pick you up after school so we can go see your mom."

"Can we get Panera for dinner on the way home?" Kimber asked.

"Sure." She held her arms out wide. "Can I have a hug before you get on the bus?" Kaden glanced furtively at the kids waiting to board, then looked at her like she had the plague. "I guess that means no goodbye kiss, either?"

She bit back a laugh when he pivoted and hurried to the bus.

"I don't mind," Kimber said as she threw her arms around Denise's waist.

"Thanks, doodlebug. Have a good day at school."

"I will." She skipped a few steps before joining the line of kids getting on the bus.

Kaden paused at the foot of the steps and raised a hand in a half wave. At least she got that.

A prickle of unease crawled up her spine and the hair on the back of her neck stood on end. All amusement fled. She kept her composure as the bus pulled away. Using the vehicle's motion, she turned as if she were watching it, but scanned from one end of the street to the other.

There. Two streets down, on the other side of the road, a man sat on a black Harley-Davidson motorcycle. The pipes rumbled with their distinct sound as he revved the throttle, pulling out two cars behind the bus. She held her breath until the rider kept going straight when the bus turned right, but he turned his head and watched the bus when he passed the turn. Then he roared off down the road, over the crest of the hill, and out of sight.

She licked her lips and her palm itched. *Don't freak out. They're safe on the bus and at school. It's just a coincidence.*

A lot of people in the area rode motorcycles—there was nothing unusual about seeing one. The patch on the back of the vest was a different story.

"AGENT NOLTON, YOU HAVE THE FLOOR."

Chris self-consciously smoothed his tie. The tailored suit fit him perfectly and he knew he looked the part of the professional agent—if only he felt it. A month ago, he'd been wearing a t-shirt that, if he'd been lucky, had been washed sometime in the previous week. He'd been more comfortable in the scrungy tee.

Clearing his throat, he pushed down his nerves. "Good morning, Director. As a result of the simultaneous operations along the interstate eighty-five corridor in North Carolina and Georgia, we've severely disrupted the Southern Anarchist's distribution lines."

The brief summarizing the operation took only fifteen minutes, but he had sweat trickling down between his shoulder blades before he was finished. He was the guy who got shit done— he hated being the monkey in the suit playing for the audience.

"What is the situation with Edward Perry?" Director Wilkins asked.

Eddie Perry's release and disappearance hadn't been covered during the brief. He wasn't sure if he should be impressed she was up to speed on the situation, or pissed off he'd spent fifteen minutes telling her shit she already knew. "Ma'am, Eddie Perry was released from jail approximately three weeks ago and has skipped parole. Several sources have reported that he's shown up at some of the old Anarchist stomping grounds, but otherwise no one has had verified contact with him."

"Is he looking to take back his former position in the Anarchists? This would be a good time for a power grab."

"We don't have a good handle on that information yet. It doesn't appear that he's trying to rally any of the old guard still left and newer members of the gang that weren't caught up in the arrests don't know him. They might not trust him."

"Family?" she asked. Her steely blue eyes met his. She already knew the answer to her question. What he wanted to know was what her plans were for the information.

"His former wife is terminally ill and in hospice."

She didn't move an inch. If her shoulder-length gray hair didn't move from the air conditioning current, he might have thought she was a statue. "And?"

"They have two children. Our assessment is that the kids haven't had any contact with their father."

Phil looked at him sharply and leaned forward on the table. "Ma'am, we do believe Eddie Perry was attempting to make contact with his kids. He'd been calling his ex-wife's house."

The Director looked from Phil to Chris. "Is that true?"

"Yes, but until three weeks ago, they believed he was dead. It's my understanding the remaining family has no desire to reestablish contact and are working to keep the kids unaware of who their father is."

"Do we know what the plan is for the kids since the ex is

terminal?" Her question was cold and calculated and her voice held no inflection of emotion or empathy. Maybe it was years of being a woman in a male-dominated field. Maybe she was just the coldhearted hard-ass rumor pegged her for.

"Her first cousin is taking care of the children at the moment," Phil said. "We're not sure about…after."

Chris looked down at the conference table, a heavy dose of guilt niggling the back of his mind. He hadn't told Phil that Denise was their guardian. He wasn't sure why he'd withheld the information other than Phil not knowing who Denise was to him. Not that he had a reason to hide it, but the whole conversation turned his stomach and left him cold.

"What do we know about the ex?"

Phil pulled one of the open file folders closer. "What little background we have on Sarah Perry prior to Eddie being arrested is minimal. Her aunt and uncle petitioned the courts for full custody when she was eleven. Her uncle was in the Army and they moved out of North Carolina shortly after. The family moved back at some point since she graduated from high school locally and went to Fayetteville State University for her teaching degree. Except for the run in when Eddie Perry was arrested, everything else is squeaky clean. Not even a parking ticket."

"What is the likelihood she knows Eddie Perry's whereabouts?" Director Wilkins asked.

"Judging by the cousin's reaction when we asked her to leave the phone line in place? Zero to none," Chris said.

She nodded once. "Find out what hospital Sarah Perry is in and see if you can get in to talk to her. Maybe she can provide some background information on Eddie that we don't have. It might give us an idea of where he'd go—who he'd reach out to for help. And keep an eye on the kids."

"Full-time surveillance?" Phil asked.

"No, but talk to the cousin. Get her cooperation. If Eddie Perry wants his kids, he'll go after them. All we have to do is wait."

Chris held in the breath he wanted to blow out. That was easier said than done. Maybe Jase and Bree would be willing to run interference for him.

The director stood and smoothed down her skirt. "Thank you for the update, agents. Keep me informed of any changes."

He and Phil murmured their assent as she left the conference room.

Special Agent Dickson shook his hand and clapped him on the shoulder. "Good job."

Chris nodded. "Thank you." He shut down the computer and gathered up his notes.

Phil waited for him in the doorway. "Where'd you get the information that the family was trying to keep the kids away from Eddie?"

He looked over his shoulder and led the way to their shared cubicle. Setting the files down, he loosened his tie. "Remember the woman I was seeing before I went undercover?"

"Vaguely, yeah." He leaned against Chris's desk and crossed one ankle over the other.

Leaning back in his chair, Chris laced his fingers together over his stomach. "She's Sarah Perry's cousin."

"You're joking?"

He shook his head slowly. "She's also the designated guardian of Sarah Perry's children for…after."

Phil's head dropped down, then rose again. "Jesus, man. Are you serious?"

"Yeah."

"Are you still seeing her?"

"No. Disappearing without a word kind of put the kibosh on that whole situation."

"The note you asked about," he said with a grimace.

"Yeah."

"Shit, man, I'm sorry."

Chris shrugged, trying for a level of indifference he in no way felt. "Shit happens."

"You get this complicates things, right? Even if you aren't seeing her anymore."

"Yeah, Phil. I get it." He sure as hell didn't need it rubbed in.

Phil scrubbed a hand over his face. "Do you know what hospital Sarah's in?"

"Cape Fear Cancer Center." Jase had shared that information.

Phil sat at his desk and typed sharply on his keyboard, then snatched up the phone handset and punched at the numbers. Chris knew his partner well enough to know he was upset Chris had kept this information from him. He wouldn't have done anything differently. He wasn't going to be pulled off this investigation. Cradle to grave and he was going to see it to the end of the Southern Anarchists. Andrew and Teresa had been murdered while undercover investigating theses fuckers and their families deserved that much.

He picked up his phone from the desk and unlocked it, opening it to the photo app. The only picture in the gallery was one he'd managed to retrieve from his back-up after getting a new phone. He'd snuck the photo of Denise while she'd slept. Half on her stomach, clutching a pillow with one leg bent and out of the sheet that seemed to hang precariously onto her lower back, it was the most relaxed he'd ever seen her. It had made him realize she was always on guard, even in sleep a small frown tugged at the corners of her mouth.

How could he get her to trust him again? Not due to the case or because he needed information, but because he needed her. He'd never needed a woman before. Never wondered what they were doing. This mission had been the first time he'd felt like he'd left something behind, something he missed and looked forward to returning to. That sure as shit didn't go according to plan.

The dent he'd made in her fortress of solitude was long gone. Patched up and smoothed over as if he'd never even scratched the surface. Her walls were stronger now for having been weakened and repaired, like a broken bone that had knitted back together, especially since she had something besides herself to guard and protect. It wasn't just emotional now, he had no doubt she would physically put herself in front of those kids. Anything he said or did at this point would be viewed with suspicion.

He couldn't even blame her. He'd probably do the same in her position.

"Fuck."

Chris flinched and locked his phone, placing it facedown on his desk as if he were a teenager whose mom had caught him looking at his dad's porn magazines.

Phil was leaned back in his chair, head resting on the back, digging the heels of his hands into his eyes.

"What?" Chris asked.

His partner dropped his hands. "Talking to Sarah Perry isn't going to be an option."

Dread uncoiled in Chris's belly, an evil and insidious snake poised to strike at the slightest provocation. He knew the answer, but asked anyway. "Why?"

"Sarah Perry passed away early this morning."

CHAPTER 7

*U*nder a low, heavy blanket of dark and rolling clouds, Chris wove through the headstones toward the group of people clustered around the casket and joined Jase and Bree toward the back of the crowd.

"Thank you for coming," Bree said. She squeezed his arm and kissed him on the cheek.

"I wasn't sure if it was the right thing to do, all things considered." He hadn't attended the memorial service. That felt like overstepping his bounds. He'd only agreed to the funeral because Bree had asked him to attend.

"Of course it's the right thing. You're still her friend."

Was he though? Denise had made it pretty clear she didn't want anything else to do with him. While she hadn't said the words *stay away*, she definitely gave a *fuck off* vibe.

The minister opened the funeral with a prayer and the low murmurs ceased. He zeroed in on Denise, seated in the front row reserved for family. Kaden sat on her lap, his face buried in her shoulder. And older woman to the left held Kimber and the man next to her rubbed the little girl's back. Her parents, judging by the resemblance. She had her mother's bone structure and her father's eyes. They were a handsome couple, so it was no wonder Denise was beautiful—even with the tension lines around her eyes and mouth.

He was surprised Sprocket wasn't pawing at her. Shifting to see the ground at her feet, he didn't find the dog. He leaned closer to Bree. "Where's Sprocket?"

Her mouth pinched tight. "Sarah's best friend thought a dog at a funeral would be undignified," she whispered.

"And Denise went along with that?"

Bree gave him an enigmatic look, then turned back to the service. "She's trying this new thing where she doesn't tell people to fuck off."

He blinked, trying to get his head around that scenario. "How's that working so far?"

"I'm surprised she hasn't cracked a molar."

Looking back at Denise, he watched the muscles at the corner of her jaw clench and unclench. She'd locked herself down tight. He had a sneaking suspicion she was doing it for the kids.

Her gaze found his, her eyes bright and shiny. She blinked and one errant tear fell to her cheek. She brushed it away angrily and looked back at the casket.

If he could have punched himself in the face right then, he would have. Fuck, he was an asshole. His determination to get back in her good graces was selfish and putting more stress on her when it was the last thing he needed.

The lead weight of defeat settled over him. He had to back off and give her the space she needed to take care of her family without any unnecessary distractions. Like him and questioning his motives. Between taking off without a word, the current investigation, and Sarah's death, he'd lost any chance he'd ever had with her. Maybe one day they could be friends and he'd be able to look at her without thinking he'd lost something irreplaceable, but it wasn't going to be today.

~

DENISE'S FACE hurt from keeping the fake, sympathetic smile in place. There were too many people in her—Sarah's living room. Extended family, friends of the family, Sarah's friends and coworkers. Hell, even some of her former students and parents had come to the funeral and now the wake. The press of bodies was as stifling as the humidity from the early season storm brewing outside and an enormous pressure filled her chest.

Sarah was loved, there was no doubt about that, which made her death that much more unfair. And made Denise that much angrier. She was close to her limit and if one more person asked her how she was holding up, or told her she was a saint for taking in the poor orphaned children of her dead cousin, she might throat punch them. Sprocket pawed at her foot and leaned harder against her, causing her to shift her weight over half a step. She reached down and absentmindedly scratched her dog's ear, fighting to keep her breathing even and steady.

"Hey." Bree held out a glass of sparkling water.

"I'm not thirsty."

"It's vodka soda."

"God, I love you." Denise accepted the glass and took a long, bracing drink.

"I figured you could use it. You're looking kind of stabby."

She grimaced. "I thought I was hiding it better than that."

"You're probably fooling everyone who doesn't know you as well as I do." She stared down at her own glass. "Chris mentioned you looked like you could use a drink."

Denise sighed. She'd seen him at the funeral, but hadn't spoken with him. Even with the small glances she'd stolen, it was hard to miss how good he looked in a suit. "He's only here because the FBI was hoping Eddie would show up."

"Actually, that's not true. Well, it may have been a bonus, but I asked him to come to the funeral."

She lowered her glass and stared at Bree. "Why?"

Her best friend gave her a *you're being dense* look. "Because regardless of what happened between you two, he still cares about you. He asks how you're doing every time I see him. And not as an FBI agent. I knew today was going to be hard for you and I knew you'd need all the support you could get. He's here for the same reason Gran was—to support you."

Not for the first time that day, tears gathered in the corners of her eyes. She blinked them away, unwilling to show that much weakness in a room full of strangers.

Bree rubbed her upper arm. "I didn't mean to upset you."

She nodded sharply. "I know. I just—I can't deal with anything else right now." She took a large sip from her drink.

"Please tell me there's alcohol in that glass," her mom said as she joined them.

Denise handed the glass over and watched as her mom drained its contents.

"Don't tell your father. He'll be mad I didn't share." She looked at Bree. "Hello, dear. That was rather rude of me."

Bree grinned. "That's okay, Karen. I completely understand. Why aren't we drinking?"

Her mom let out a long-suffering sigh. "Sarah's best friend, Melissa, thought it would be inappropriate with so many of Sarah's students coming. Might give them the wrong impression of how to handle grief."

Denise scoffed. "She should have had it at her place then." She liked Melissa, in small doses, but she was rather uptight and proper.

"The thought crossed my mind, but she lives in a one-bedroom apartment and we're Sarah's family. It wouldn't have been right."

Looking around at all the people crammed into her cousin's small house, Denise said, "There's not that much more room here. That's why we should have kept it to family and close friends."

"Don't you start. It's bad enough your father's bitching about, and I quote, 'All the damn people in this tiny-ass house.'" Tears welled up in her eyes and spilled down her cheeks.

"Mom?"

"And now I'm out-numbered." Her mom threw her hands up in a hopeless gesture. "Neither you nor your father are emotional. I could always count on Sarah to cry during sappy movies with me." A sob shook her shoulders.

"Oh, Mom." Denise pulled her into a hug, resting her cheek on the top of her head. "I'll watch sappy movies with you."

"But you won't cry!" More sobs shook her mom's shoulders as her arms tightened around Denise.

Oh, jeez. She was never going to live down not crying during *The Notebook*. She scanned the room, searching for her dad. He must have been watching them, because he was threading his way through the mourners, heading their direction.

When he reached them, he gathered her mom in his arms and tucked her against his chest. At six-foot-three, he towered over her five-foot-five mom.

"Hi, Bree. Sorry about the waterworks," he said.

"That's okay, Frank. It's an appropriate day for waterworks."

"Yeah. I suppose it is." He swallowed hard and cleared his throat.

She heard the catch in his voice. She and her dad may not cry as much as Sarah and her mom, but that didn't mean they didn't feel it just as much.

Denise felt a tap on her hip and looked over, then down. "Hey, buddy. What's up?"

"I want to lay down," Kaden said.

"Okay." Poor guy had to be exhausted.

"Will you lay with me?" He'd asked for her to lie with him while he fell asleep every night since she'd told them their mom had died. If he didn't climb into bed with her, he was in bed with Kimber when she went to wake them in the morning.

"Sure, buddy." She took his hand. "I'll come back out as soon as he's asleep," she said to her dad.

"Don't worry about it. You look like you're handling this crowd about as well as I am. I'm going to tell people they should leave before the storm breaks."

Her mom lifted her head from her dad's chest, her eyes red and puffy. "Jesus, Frank. You can't kick people out."

He glared down at her. "I'm going to kindly suggest they leave for safety reasons. Me kicking them out would be to tell them to get the fuck out of my daughter's house."

"Alrighty, then. I'm going to take little ears to lie down. Let Kimber know where we are in case she wants to cuddle with us."

She took Kaden's hand and weaved through the clusters of people, giving a tight smile to everyone who said they were sorry for her loss along the way. They were probably sincere. Maybe some of them had suffered their own loss at some point, but she couldn't deal with any more people today. She was peopled out.

Thankfully, Kaden gave her the perfect excuse not to stop and exchange pleasantries. Against her will, she cast a look over her shoulder to where she'd last seen Chris. She'd been aware of him all afternoon. He'd mumbled the standard prayers along with everyone else, but she'd known he watched her the entire time. Just like he watched her ushering Kaden through the crowd. The crease between his brows was prominent as he followed her with his gaze.

Once Sprocket cleared the threshold to the bedroom, she shut the door with a relieved sigh.

"Will you snuggle me?" Kaden asked, climbing onto the bed.

"Sure." She pushed away from the door and kicked off her flats. "Let's take your shoes off though."

He yanked off his shoes and dropped them to the floor. She pulled her phone from the pocket of Sprocket's vest and set it on the bedside table, then unhooked the vest from around Sprocket's chest and neck.

"Why did Sprocket have to wear her vest today?"

"Because there were so many people here who don't know her, I wanted to make sure they knew she was working and they shouldn't pet her or try to play with her."

"Oh." He sat on the bed, legs crossed, picking at his fingernails while he waited for her.

She lay down in the middle of the bed. "Hang on. My skirt's tangled." She lifted her hips and adjusted the material so it wasn't pulling at her hips. "Okay."

Kaden all but launched himself at her, tucking his head into the pocket of her shoulder, throwing an arm across her chest. She rubbed his back as best she could with the limited reach she had.

The door clicked open and Kimber entered, closing it behind her.

Denise opened her free arm and Kimber joined them on the bed, mirroring Kaden's position, resting her arm on top of Kaden's.

A few minutes passed, then her whole body rocked from the force of the sob wrenched out of Kimber. More followed and Kaden began crying as well.

Her throat tightened up and her eyes stung for what seemed like the ten-thousandth time that day. She shoved down the pain, staying strong for Kaden and Kimber. She squeezed them tight and kissed the tops of their heads. "I know, sweetie. I know."

CHAPTER 8

*D*enise stared up at the ceiling, letting the freight train of emotion and thoughts ramble through her mind. She tried not to stop on any particular one to examine it more closely because as soon as she did, she'd be overwhelmed by what the future held in store for her. Ignoring was bliss and she'd reign as the Queen of Denial for another few hours before she had to face reality. Except one thought kept pushing to the front.

Chris.

What was she supposed to do about him? He was going to be in their lives, for the near term at least, because of Eddie. Long term, he was Jase's best friend so they'd always run into each other. She was grown-up enough to admit her feelings were hurt. Regardless of what he said, she had been an afterthought. He'd put his job first. Maybe she expected too much. Maybe she wanted too much. She was almost childish enough to want to stamp her foot and yell *I don't care*. For once in her adult life, she wanted to be first.

Her phone vibrated on the bedside table and she reached for it. A severe thunderstorm warning flashed across the screen.

Of course. Because she had the worst luck in the world. Laying with the kids, she'd hoped the low thunder she'd heard was simply a passing storm and the clouds that had cast a depressing pall over the funeral would break gently. At least it wasn't a tornado warning.

She needed to make sure the generator was connected at the rescue and check on the dogs. A few of the boarders were highly anxious and they had to be placed with other dogs or they could hurt themselves trying to escape from their pens. One owner had brought a hug vest specifically for bad weather.

Checking that both kids were asleep, she eased out from under them and scooted off the end of the bed. Pulling her dress over her head, she threw it toward the hamper and bent down to rummage in her suitcase.

Living out of a suitcase sucked, but she hadn't wanted to move any of Sarah's clothes to make room for her own. It hadn't seemed right while she'd been alive. Now, it was just depressing. Final in a way she couldn't face yet. Maybe her mom would be up for it. If not, Bree would probably help her.

Her rain boots were back at her apartment, so she slipped into her flip-flops. Patting the end of the bed she said, "Up." Sprocket jumped onto the bed and sat.

She scratched her behind the ears. "Good girl. Stay with K-Squared." Sprocket licked Denise's chin, then low-crawled up the bed until she was between Kimber and Kaden, resting her head on her paws.

She slipped out the door and braced for the onslaught of people. A sigh of relief escaped when she found only her parents, one of her dad's sisters, and Bree and Jase. And Chris. A small flame of hope flared to life. Maybe he'd stayed out of concern for her. Or maybe he stayed because he was FBI and he had VIP access to the party.

The flame sputtered and died as the dull ache in her chest throbbed. She ignored it, just like every other time she'd felt it.

"Hey, honey," her mom said, opening her arms to Denise. "Are the kids asleep?"

She hugged her mom. "Yeah. I need to go to the rescue to check on some of the dogs and make sure the generator is hooked up in case the storm knocks out the power. Can you stay for a while?"

"Well, we were going to go back to the hotel with your aunt Tammy. I supposed I can stay while your dad takes her back to the hotel and then comes back for me."

"We can stay," Bree said.

Denise leaned against the counter. "Are you sure?"

"Of course. We don't have anywhere else to be tonight and there's no reason for your dad to make two trips. And I think Tammy's ready to go." She nodded to the couch.

Her aunt had her head propped on her fist on the arm of the couch, eyes closed with her mouth slightly open.

"If you really don't mind, we would appreciate it," her dad said.

"We don't mind." Bree slipped her arm around Jase's waist.

Denise caught the slight squeeze she gave his waist and narrowed her eyes at Bree. She was up to something, but she didn't have the time to worry about it.

"I'll let you guys fight it out," she said. "Make sure you get it on video if it comes to blows." She grabbed her keys from the hook by the door. Chris's gaze following her out an almost tangible weight.

CHRIS CAUGHT Jase starring up at the ceiling and shaking his head. He pressed his lips together to hide his amusement at his friend's exasperation.

"I shouldn't be too long," Denise said.

"Take your time," Bree said.

"We'll stay for a few more minutes," her mom said. "I'll try to find room for all this food." She gestured to plastic storage containers stacked on the short counters.

"I can't believe people still do that," Denise said. "Tell Aunt Tammy I'll talk to her tomorrow." She hugged her parents and Bree.

He caught the eye flick his way, but didn't know what to make of it. It was cautious and flirtatious at the same time—an involuntary eye spasm in his direction.

Defeat beat down on him with its meaty fists. All he'd wanted to do all day was touch her. Comfort her. Tell her he was there for her and it would eventually be alright. That she was one of the strongest people he knew and she had this. Maybe one day he could get her to trust him again, but at that moment he wasn't holding out hope. She could hardly look at him.

"This is a lot of food," Bree said.

Karen glanced between the two counters. "I know. I hope I can make room for it all. I'd hate for any of it to go to waste."

"Did anyone bring anything good or is it all casserole?" Frank asked.

"I think it's mostly casserole," Karen said.

"Gross. Throw that crap out. The kids won't eat it anyway."

"Frank—"

Thunder exploded over their heads, followed quickly by a bright flash of lightning and they all flinched.

"You guys should go before the storm gets really bad," Bree said.

Another crack of thunder rent the air and lightning lit up the dark sky visible through the small kitchen window. The lights flashed, but stayed on.

"Come on. Let's get in the car and on the road," Frank said.

"Hang on. Sarah keeps candles in the kitchen." Karen pulled open a drawer and pulled out several small candles and a box of matches. She closed the drawer and looked down at the counter. "Kept. She kept them here."

She brushed a tear away and took a bracing breath. "Let's go." She turned and hugged Bree. "Tell Denise and kids we'll see them tomorrow."

"I will," Bree said.

Chris remained leaning against the counter and swirled the last of the tea in his glass. It was time for him to go as well. It would be weird if he hung out with Jase and Bree to wait for Denise to return. He couldn't make the offer to stay in case the kids woke up since they barely knew him. Besides, it went against the decision he'd made only a short while ago to give Denise her space.

He finished the last of his drink and placed the glass in the sink. "I'm going to head out," he told them when they returned to the kitchen.

"You sure? You can hang out here for a while," Bree said.

"No. I'm going to go before the storm gets worse. I'd say thanks for having me, but...well."

Bree nodded. "Yeah. But thank you for coming anyway."

He shook hands with Jase and dashed out to his truck, parked several houses down the street. A driving rain pelted him with fat drops of water, soaking him through his suit jacket. Unlocking his truck, he launched himself into the driver's seat and slammed the door. A blast of cool air chilled him when he started the truck and he adjusted the vents away from him.

He loved the south, but damn there were times he could do without the weather. Peeling his jacket down his arms, he threw it into the back seat and loosened his tie. His shirt was just as sopping, so he peeled that off with the tie, leaving him in nothing but his v-neck undershirt. His dress shoes were probably ruined as well.

He glanced over the seat to see if he had an extra bag in the back. Murphy apparently didn't have anything against hunters because he found a pair of hiking boots in a duffel on the back seat. There wasn't much he could do about his wet feet, but at least they weren't encased in wet socks anymore.

Gripping the steering wheel, he tried to convince himself he was waiting for the windshield to finish defogging and not trying to think of an excuse to go after Denise. She didn't need him and she'd made that crystal clear. Shaking his head, he checked his mirror and pulled onto the street. He'd help her by finding Eddie Perry and putting him back in jail.

Fifteen minutes later, the wipers were on full speed and barely keeping the windshield clear enough for him to see. His phone rang and he answered it with the Bluetooth button on the dash. "This is Nolton."

"Chris? It's Bree."

He could barely hear her over the pounding rain on the metal of his truck.

"Is something wrong?"

"Can you check on Denise?" she asked. "I've texted her a couple of times, but she hasn't answered me."

"Uh. I don't think I'm the best person to do that, all things considered."

"Right now, you're the only one that can. Jase isn't going to let me drive out there by myself in this weather."

There was a short pause and he could hear Jase's voice, but not what he was saying.

"I need to be here in case the kids wake up since they don't know Jase as well."

"Bree—"

"Please, Chris. She didn't take Sprocket with her and she's also not in a good place. Plus, if something happens to her in the storm, no one is there to help her. I need some peace of mind and to know she's okay. Please."

Damn. Looked like he had a reason to go after her after all.

"Yeah. I'll check on her."

CHAPTER 9

*D*enise held the trembling dog away from her as anxiety caused it to empty its bladder. It was the second dog that had done that. She hadn't been quick enough with the first dog and now she reeked of piss.

Blowing out a breath through clenched teeth, she set the dog down in the pen and it ran to the corner to curl up on the mat with the other two dogs already huddled together.

On a positive note, most of it should wash off in the torrential downpour she had to walk through to get back to her apartment.

Perfect fucking ending to a perfect fucking day.

The dog seemed to calm down as the others welcomed her and she arranged herself on the pile. Even the damn dogs had someone to comfort them. She had...her. Her nose began to sting and her bottom lip trembled. Turning on her heel, she headed to the barn door. Setting the lights on low, she stepped through the smaller man-door, making sure to lock it behind her.

The sheets of rain drenched her within moments. A few steps into the yard, thunder crashed overhead.

"Fuck!" Mother Nature's violence fed the anger roiling inside her, primer on the detonation cord waiting for an inopportune

61

moment to set off the explosion she was desperately trying to keep contained.

But it wasn't fucking fair. Sarah was loving and kind and forgiving and had finally been in a good place in her life. She had two smart, beautiful kids who didn't deserve to lose their mom to cancer.

Denise was halfway across the yard when lightning split the sky and struck a tree in the field next to the barn.

Fists clenched at her side, she screamed into the storm. Everything came crashing down—the anger, the pain, the fear, and uncertainty pressed mercilessly down on her and she couldn't bear the weight of it any longer. Her knees buckled and she sank to the ground.

Violent sobs forced their way out of her chest. The storm raged and crashed around her, echoing the one inside her. A small, rational section of her brain told her to get her dumb ass up and out of the rain, but she couldn't make her limbs move. Couldn't find the strength to keep pushing forward.

"Denise! Denise!"

Hands grabbed her upper arms, jerking her out of her stupor.

Surging to her feet, she fought the person holding her, pushing away from him.

"Denise, it's Chris!"

She didn't care. She needed to lash out and hurt something—someone. Use her fists to transfer this pain and anger away from her onto someone else.

Her fist connected with a hard wall of flesh, followed by a muffled, "Oomph."

"You wanna let it out?" he shouted. "Have at it."

"Fuck you!" She threw a left jab, followed by a right hook to his jaw, snapping his head to the side.

He turned his head back and laughed. "That's it?"

"Fuck! You!" She shoved him and forced him back a step.

He took two forward, crowding into her space. The thin material of his t-shirt molded to his chest and abs while water dripped from his face. He held his arms out to the side, daring her to hit him again. "Come on, Denise. I know you can do better than that. Give me your worst."

Something inside her broke. Shattered. She didn't want to do her worst. She didn't want to keep feeling this way. Taking a shuddering breath, she closed the distance between them and grabbed the sides of his face, pulling his mouth down to hers.

He flinched and, for a few heartbeats, she worried he wouldn't respond. As she made the decision to pull away, his arms banded tightly around her and he opened his mouth, his tongue thrusting into hers.

Thank God. This was what she wanted to feel. Comfort and care from another person, in the touch and caress given by a lover. Given by Chris. Pressing her body against his, she wrapped her arms around his neck.

Pulling back slightly, he said, "Up", then sealed his mouth back to hers. He bent slightly and hefted her weight.

Denise wrapped her legs around his waist, locking her water-filled boots together behind his back. Rain seeped past her lips and mingled with their kiss, making it wetter and hotter. His wide-legged pace ate up the distance across the yard and he was climbing the stairs in mere seconds.

Halfway up, he stumbled on a step. Sharp wood risers dug into her back and hips when he fell forward, all but dropping her on the stairs.

"Ow! Shit. Sorry." He braced himself above her, blocking the rain from falling into her eyes. "You okay?"

"I think so," she said. Pain radiated from the center of her back and hips where she'd landed, but the bruises would be worth it tomorrow.

"We should probably walk up normally."

"Yeah."

"I don't want to give you room to think." He used a finger to hook a wet strand of hair off her cheek.

"About what?"

"About whatever it is you think about that makes you shut down."

His gaze was too intense. She looked at his mouth, his lips wet from the rain and their kiss. All she had to do was say the word and he would walk away. He'd pretend he hadn't found her losing her shit in the middle of a thunderstorm. But how many times could she push him away before he stayed away for good? She was so tired of being alone. Even when she went back to Sarah's and Kaden and Kimber, she'd still be alone.

She looked back up. Chris waited patiently while cold rain pounded onto his back. "I'm not going to shut down."

He hesitated, as if he was going to ask her something, but decided against it. She almost asked him *what*, but the same hesitation stopped her.

What about tomorrow?

She didn't want to think about tomorrow when she had to face the reality of being a single parent and all that entailed. Right now, she just wanted to think about him and the next few moments.

Curling up, she kissed him. His hand cradled the back of her head as he slanted his mouth over hers. They stayed there until another rumble of thunder rolled over their heads. She pulled away. "No thinking. For the next ten minutes, at least."

He scowled at her. "Ten minutes, my ass. Up." Pushing away from the stairs, he helped her stand then turned her and prodded her up to the landing.

She pulled her wet feet out of her boots and pushed open the door. Spinning as soon as she cleared the threshold, she threw herself into Chris's arms, latching onto his mouth once more. He shifted their bodies so he could close the door, stumbling back against it as he took her weight.

"Shoes," he mumbled against her lips.

She stepped back and watched him bend at the waist to untie his hiking boots. He'd changed out of his suit at some point. Water pooled at their feet as it dripped from their bodies. Tugging at her shirt, she shimmied out of the clinging material, dropping it in a sopping pile. He paused and looked at her shirt, then sped up his movements.

"Fucking laces are knotted," he muttered. He reached into his back pocket and a pulled out a knife. Flipping it open, he slid it under the laces of his right shoe and flicked his wrist. He closed the blade and stood while kicking out of his boots.

"Eager much?"

"Fuck, yes."

She glanced up from the stuck zipper she was trying to work down. His gaze was fixed on her chest. She noted her simple white bra had become see through. He'd apparently noticed the same thing.

He lunged at her, taking her to the ground in a controlled move while his mouth latched onto her nipple. Sweet baby Jesus, he'd better be able to get her jeans off. Heat radiated from him, warming her front while the cool floor under her caused her to shiver.

Or maybe it was all him. He pulled the cup of her bra down, flicking her pebbled nipple with his tongue. She moaned and thrust her hips against him. He tugged at her pants, wrenching at the zipper until it gave, then peeled them down her legs. On the way back up he put his hot, open mouth on the exposed skin of her hip, sucking briefly before licking the same spot.

Her eyes closed and she rolled her hips up, pressing harder against his mouth. For once she wished she was the type of woman who wore sexy, lacy underwear instead of simple, cotton briefs.

"I'm about to be doin' a whole lot better," Chris said.

"What?" She popped her head up in confusion.

He nuzzled the juncture of her thighs. "Your underwear says, 'How you doin'?' I was letting you know, I'm about to be a whole lot better. So are you." His teeth scraped against her clit, through her underwear.

Liquid warmth spread up and out. "Chris, I want to feel you inside me."

"You will. Just as soon as I can get out of these jeans." His movements were frenzied, pushing the wet material of his pants past his thighs.

She lifted her hips and shoved her underwear down to her knees, managing to free one leg from the constricting material. His cock sprang forward and the warm, hard length rested against the inside of her thigh. His hands seemed to be everywhere at once—her butt, her breast, her hip—as if he wanted to touch all of her at one time. Wrapping her hand around him, she stroked from the base to the tip, rubbing her thumb through the drop of moisture at the tip.

He groaned and one of his hands briefly disappeared behind his back and returned holding a condom. He ripped the packet with his teeth, then pushed her hand out of the way while he rolled it on. Lining himself up with her entrance, he pushed forward, bottoming out in one hard thrust.

She hissed against the invasion and the sting. Surrounded. Engulfed. As if an ocean wave had crashed over her, enveloping her in its peaceful silence all while threatening never to release her from its powerful grasp. Dropping his face into the hollow of her shoulder, he stayed still, buried to the hilt. His lips soft and gentle against the sensitive skin of her neck while he throbbed inside her, his heartbeat keeping time with hers, a clock ticking down to some kind of explosion. One that had the power to cleanse or destroy.

It may have been seconds or hours, but just as she reached her threshold and was ready to push him away and retreat to her bedroom, he moved. Slow at first, as if he needed a moment to find his rhythm, then fast, hard, and uncontrolled. He hooked an arm under her leg and moved it to his shoulder, tilting her pelvis up, which allowed him even further into her core. Pushing up, he pistoned his hips with enough force she began to inch across the floor. She held on to his back and shoulders, wrapping her other leg high around his ass.

He looked down at where they were joined. She followed his gaze and watched him thrust in and out. Her breathing quickened as she anticipated each time he disappeared into her tight sheath, savoring the brief press against her clit, straining for more contact. More pressure. Something to help push her over the precipice she hovered on.

He dropped down to his elbows, obscuring her view. His hands cupped the sides of her face, his thumbs brushing the tops of her cheeks. She looked into his eyes and promptly closed hers.

"Denise."

She opened her eyes.

"Stay with me."

Her brows pinched together, unsure of the meaning in his gaze. It unnerved her. There was something...more. Something she wasn't ready to face.

He thumbed her clit, putting just the right amount of pressure on the hood. There it was, that feeling coalescing in the very center of her. Her eyelids fluttered shut as she concentrated on letting her orgasm take her.

"Eyes open, Denise."

Her eyes snapped open and immediately clashed with his. The damn broke—in more ways than one. Tears leaked from the corners of her eyes as she came. The wave of release pushing everything up and out of her.

She closed her eyes and turned her head away, hardly aware of whether Chris came with her or after her. Dropping her leg, she waited for him to finish. She felt like an asshole, but she needed him to be done and to leave her alone. He kissed her cheek and her temple. Trying to hold it in only made it worse and she began to tremble.

"Shhh. It's okay."

But it wasn't. Her body heaved with the force of her crying. She covered her face with her hands and curled onto her side, pulling her legs up close to her body.

"Shit. Denise, please talk to me."

She shook her head. "Just go."

"Fuck!" A chill descended when he stood and she heard the rustling of his jeans.

He'd done exactly what she'd asked him to do. So why was she crying even harder now that he was gone?

CHAPTER 10

*F*uck, fuck, fuck.

    Chris pulled up his jeans, not caring that the condom was falling off his softening dick. He had bigger things to worry about. Like what the hell had set Denise off right after they'd had sex. Had he hurt her? Did she regret what they'd done? Should he have taken his time and gotten her into her bedroom? Shit, he hadn't even been able to get his pants off and her underwear still hung on one ankle.

Regardless, he couldn't leave her like that, curled up in the fetal position on the cold floor of her entryway. They hadn't even made it to the living room. She could hate him later for ignoring her order to leave.

Squatting down, he hooked an arm under her legs and shoulders and scooped her up, cradling her to his chest. She cried almost uncontrollably and it tore him apart. He carried her into her bedroom and laid her down on the bed. She didn't acknowledge him or her change in position.

Indecisive, he stood by the bed warring with his earlier decision to leave her alone and unwilling to leave her vulnerable. Fuck it.

In the bathroom, he removed the condom and peeled his pants off inside-out, hanging them over the shower rod. Grabbing a hand towel from the bar on the wall, he went back into the bedroom. Denise hadn't moved, although her crying seemed to have eased up some. He cradled her head and lifted it from the pillow. With his other hand, he spread the towel out under her head and hair as best he could and folded the towel over the wet ends.

Going to the other side of the bed, he lay down behind her. He snagged the edge of the soft comforter and pulled it over them. He wrapped his arms around her and held her tight as a fresh wave of sobs escaped.

Maybe this wasn't the right thing to do. He swallowed hard. "I'll go if that's what you really want," he said softly.

She gripped his arm so tightly he'd likely have bruises in the morning. They'd go nicely with the one he was probably sporting on his jaw. Denise had a mean right hook. He released a sigh and pressed his forehead to the back of her neck, the tension leaving his body. He hadn't realized how much he wanted her to want him to stay until that moment. He had no idea what would happen tomorrow, but she needed him in that moment, whether she could admit it or not. If this was all she needed, so be it. This was what he would give her.

CHRIS JERKED awake when Denise left the bed. Watching her walk to the bathroom, he realized he hadn't taken her bra off when he'd carried her to bed. She closed the door and he released a pent-up breath. Was he supposed to leave now? The toilet flushed and he took the coward's way out—he closed his eyes and pretended to be asleep.

The bed shifted as she eased back into it, giving him her back, but pressing close to him. Cracking open his eyes, he stared at the back of her head and concentrated on keeping his breathing slow and even. She rolled to her stomach and pulled the pillow under her head.

"I was an interrogator at an Operational Detachment in Iraq," she said. "One of the ones no one admitted existed."

So much for pretending to be asleep. He half rolled on top of her, pressing his lips to the center of her back. Her chest rose and fell with each breath.

"I got involved with one of the senior interrogators. He was CIA. Older. More experienced. I was young and still naive, but I was good at my job. I was able to get information without resorting to some of the more…drastic measures, but I did that, too, when I had to."

He didn't say anything—he didn't want to interrupt her and possibly derail her story. Instead he rubbed his lips across her back, tracing her tattoo of Joan of Arc.

"Back then, they still took women and children off the objective if they missed the primary target. One night they went out for a key Al-Qaida leader but he wasn't at the target house. They brought back his sister instead and her ten-year-old son. His name was Ali. He came because he was protecting his mother's honor. Preston, the guy I was involved with, decided the sister had information on her brother's activities, so they decided to keep her in detention along with Ali. I was sent in as a friendly face to get information since it wasn't acceptable to torture women."

She paused and he couldn't help but think a guy named Preston was a pretentious asshole. He'd never hated someone so much in his life for no other reason than his name.

"After a couple of weeks, I was told to concentrate on Ali instead. The kid was funny. And smart. He picked up English really fast. I was spending a couple of hours a day with him. I didn't think he knew anything, but Preston kept pushing, telling me to use harsher tactics to get the intel they needed on his uncle.

I refused and I refused to let them do it. Threatened to go up the chain if they tried it."

She took a shuddering breath, as if preparing herself for what she was going to say next. He was afraid he knew.

"I got a Red Cross notification that Sarah was in the hospital." Her voice broke and she sniffled into the pillow. She took another deep breath. "When I got back to the base, Ali and his mom weren't there anymore. I asked and kept getting vague answers—they'd been released, they'd been transferred—no one could give me a straight answer. Finally, I confronted my roommate, who was an analyst. A few days after I left Iraq, there was a major coordinated attack on the camp. Lasted a couple of days. For some reason, Preston got it in his head that Ali knew about the attack and had information on it. He died during the interrogation. His mother committed suicide."

Jesus. He couldn't even fathom it. His team had taken young males off objectives, but they'd never taken children. They sure as hell hadn't ever interrogated a fucking kid.

"I was so angry. About everything. Eddie. Sarah. Ali. I went after Preston with a crowbar. Cracked his jaw and broke his arm. I had my gun to his head when my OIC walked in. He talked me out of putting a bullet in his head. Told me he wasn't worth my life. Preston was on a plane the next day. They came up with some story about a utility vehicle rolling over on him to explain his injuries. My boss gave me the information on the Combat Support Teams the next day."

She rubbed her face on the pillow. "The worst part was I blamed Sarah, of all people." She scoffed. "How fucked up is that?"

He rubbed his nose across her back and felt it was safe to ask, "Why did you blame Sarah?"

"She was in the hospital because of Eddie. If she'd left him like we'd urged her to, I wouldn't have had to go home and Ali would be alive.

He stroked her arm. "You don't know that. A douche canoe

like that guy would have found a way. He could have done it one night while you were sleeping or at the gym or anytime he wanted."

She stayed quiet for several minutes. Had he said the wrong thing? Had she retreated back behind her walls? He continued to caress her arm and back.

"I know," she said in a small voice. "But I didn't talk to her for almost a year. She didn't deserve that and I never said I was sorry."

Her chest heaved with her fresh tears. He had nothing. No words of wisdom to help her work through her guilt or her pain, so he held her and tried to comfort her as best he could. Eventually, her tears subsided.

"Will you tell me about her?" he asked.

"What do you want to know?"

"You guys were really close?"

"Yes. I wish we'd spent more time together when we were kids, but she was almost five years younger than I am. I was already in high school when she came to live with us. I thought it was cool, finally having a little sister, but we didn't really have a lot in common."

"Why did she live with you?"

She sighed. "Her step-father was physically abusing her."

"Like...?" Christ, how much bad luck could one person have?

"No. She wasn't sexually abused. Just physically. How horrible is that, that I have to qualify abuse by 'just physically?'"

"Pretty fucking horrible."

Denise rolled over and faced away from him. She pulled his arm over her waist and gripped his wrist. Maybe talking about these things was easier if she couldn't see him. "Her mom and my mom are sisters. We were driving to North Carolina from Florida and decided to surprise them on the way since they lived in South Carolina. Their house was trashed. No food. Garbage everywhere. I remember Sarah stank to high heaven and she couldn't remember the last time she'd had a bath. My dad lost his shit. Beat the crap out of my aunt's husband and told my aunt we were taking Sarah and she'd have to call the cops if she wanted to try to stop him. My parents went to court for custody the next year. It was uncontested."

She was playing with his fingers and he couldn't help but let his mind wander to other things he'd like her to play with, but it wasn't the time.

"I'll tell you what I can about Eddie."

"That's not why I'm here, Denise."

"I know that. Sarah worked really hard to get away from him and to give those kids the love and happiness she never really had." She shook her head. "I'll help how I can, but nothing can happen to those kids. I won't put them in a position where that's even a possibility."

He kissed the back of her head. "You won't have to."

CHAPTER 11

*D*enise blinked in the early morning light and scrunched up her swollen face. Her sinuses were stuffed and her forehead felt like someone had beaned her in the center of it a hammer. Plus, her stomach was a little queasy, probably because she hadn't had much to eat at the wake last night.

Shit. Kaden and Kimber. Grabbing for her phone on the nightstand, she unlocked it and revealed a screen full of texts from Bree.

How're the dogs?

Are you okay?

Please answer me. I'm starting to worry.

Sending the cavalry.

Then this morning: Sleep in. *Taking the kids for pancakes.*

Mortification was an ugly bedfellow. A sneak-out-the-next-morning-without-trying-to-find-your-underwear, pretend-it-never-happened kind of ugly. Holy bejeezus, she'd made an ass out of herself.

A low, snuffling snore came from behind her and she froze. *Please let that be Sprocket.* Except she'd left Sprocket with the kids.

She eased onto her back and stared at Chris still sleeping in the bed next to her. Maybe if she slunk down under the covers, she'd find a portal to a parallel dimension where she hadn't lost her shit in the middle of a thunderstorm, hadn't cried after sex, and wasn't currently fighting a wave of nausea brought on by either hunger or extreme embarrassment. It was hard to tell which was the driving force.

He'd stayed though. Even when she'd turned into a certifiable basket case. Even after she'd given him what promised to be an impressive black eye.

He rolled to his stomach and bunched the pillow under his head. Blinking his eyes a few times, he finally left them cracked in a sultry, half-open gaze.

"Morning," he mumbled. "What time is it?"

"Almost eight."

"M'kay. Thirty more minutes." He shut his eyes again.

There was no stopping the smile at his adorableness.

"You're staring at me."

"Just looking," she said.

A few seconds passed and he blinked his eyes and closed them again.

"What happened to your leg?" she asked. The scar was still red and not one he'd had before he left.

He sighed and turned to his side to face her, bunching the pillow under his head. "We had two agents undercover with the Anarchists. They'd missed a couple of check-ins, which was unusual. I was sent in as the brother of one of the agents. My cover was I was trying to find him because our dad was sick. I kept getting the runaround on where my agents were."

His eyes were on her, but his gaze was focused inward like he was watching the reel of events play in his mind while giving her the highlights. "Their bodies turned up in a landfill. They'd both been shot execution-style and thrown away like garbage. One of the agents was a woman."

The last statement hung in the air. He didn't elaborate. He didn't need to. This conversation had gotten way heavier than she'd intended.

He swallowed hard. "We weren't sure if my cover had been blown, so we set up the raid a few days after they were found." Rolling to his back, he scrubbed a hand over his face. "It went ugly, fast. I took a hatchet to the knee."

She winched and sucked in a breath.

He looked back at her. "Surgeon said if it hadn't been dull or had gone half an inch left or right, it would have really fucked up my knee. Instead, it cut through to the kneecap. Thirty-four stitches later, I've got an awesome scar and a fucked-up story."

"I'm sorry." There was nothing more to say. It sucked that he'd lost two agents and had been injured, but selfishly it didn't assuage the pain at being abandoned with no word. Maybe that made her a bad person.

He rolled back to his side. "So am I. I didn't mean to ghost. When I got the word I was going in, I was ordered to go radio silent. We have protocols in place to make sure our covers can't be tracked to our real lives, including shutting down all forms of communication."

It was her turn to drop her gaze. "I got it." Still didn't make it hurt any less.

"Denise." His voice was soft and gravely and raised goose-bumps on her arms as if he'd dragged the tips of his fingers across her skin.

"It's alright, Chris."

"It's not."

She looked up. "But it'll probably happen again."

"Maybe."

There was the problem. He couldn't say for sure one way or the other. More than likely it would happen again. Maybe not with her, but with someone.

At the thought of him telling someone else he had to go, a

bright, hot wave of jealousy surged through her from out of nowhere. The suddenness of her rage caught her off guard and she jerked.

A furrow appeared between his brows. "You okay?"

She pressed her lips together. "Mmm hmm. Muscle spasm."

"You sure?"

"Yeah. Why did you join the Army first? Why not go straight to college?" She wanted to know everything about him with an urgency she hadn't felt before. Before had been casual and lazy— they'd had all the time in the world. Now she knew that wasn't true.

"No money. My grades weren't good enough for an academic scholarship and I wasn't good enough at any sport to get a scholarship. Most of my high school friends were going nowhere fast. A couple O.D.'d on meth or heroin and the Army offered me a way out. What about you? Why the Army and not college?"

"I went for about two years before I joined, but it wasn't for me. I didn't know what I wanted to do and I'd always had it in the back of my mind that I'd join. We were in Virginia and my dad got orders back to Bragg. I was going to community college and living at home. I did not want to do that in Fayetteville, so I enlisted."

The corner of his mouth quirked up. "And you ended up back here anyway."

She tucked her hands under her head. "I'd like to point out Haven Creek is a good thirty minutes away from Fayetteville," she said.

"Touché. You never wanted to finish your degree?"

"I have a Master's in Business Management."

"Really?"

Her eyebrows pinched together. "Why do you sound so surprised?"

"It's just—Well, you—I don't have anything to say around the foot in my mouth."

She smiled. "It's alright. People do it all the time."

He brushed a strand of hair away from her face. "They shouldn't. *I* shouldn't have. I should've known better than to underestimate you."

A swarm of butterflies took flight in her stomach and her muscles felt gooey. Shit. This was what girlie felt like. It'd been so long since it'd happened, she almost forgot.

"Why seven years?"

"Huh?" What was seven years?

"When we first got together you said you hadn't been with anyone in seven years. How come?"

"Oh." Warmth spread across the tops of her cheeks. "Um, the short answer is I never liked anyone enough to want to go through the hassle of it."

"Of sex?" His shocked expression was comical.

"Of any of it." She shrugged. "I either intimidated guys or they viewed me as a challenge. The limited reward was never worth the effort."

"I don't think you were meeting the right kind of guys."

"No doubt."

He shifted closer. "Thanks for thinking I was worth the effort."

She bit the inside of her cheek. "I'm sorry about last night." It was a morning for sorries.

His hand cupped the side of her face. "Don't. You have nothing to apologize for." He kissed her gently and pulled her into his arms.

It was sweet and comforting and the girlie emotions rose up inside her. She didn't know what do to with what she was feeling, so she tucked her face into his neck and simply enjoyed not having to worry about anything.

A few minutes later, he said, "I need to go to work for a few hours. You going to be okay?"

The disappointment at his announcement was why she never let the girlie emotions have free reign. "Yeah, I'll be fine." Wasn't she always?

He pressed a kiss to her forehead. "Call me if you need me."

~

DENISE HEAVED a sigh while she rubbed Sweetpea's belly and considered the options. Let someone adopt her or adopt the dog herself. It made sense really. Kaden and Kimber had been monopolizing Sprocket. She felt bad telling them no, but there were times she absolutely needed Sprocket with her. When she went grocery shopping for one. There were no delivery companies that serviced the rescue or Bree's house so that wasn't an option and, with Kimber and Kaden, neither was going late at night like she normally did to avoid the worst of the crowds. Getting the dog for K-Squared was common sense. They'd have a dog they could play with and she'd have Sprocket back. Problem solved.

The door from the reception area slammed closed. She pivoted in her crouched position to see Emily, one of her part-time employees, rushing toward her, clutching her phone.

She rose, closing and latching the kennel gate. "What's wrong?"

"Uh, there's a really scary guy here to see you. Should I call the police?"

Denise raised her eyebrows. "Scary how?"

"Just...something about him. He's got all these tattoos and..." She shuddered. "The way he looked at me. Like, guys look at me, but not like that."

"Like what?" She could see real fear in Emily's eyes. They dealt with people with tattoos all the time, including local police, so that wasn't it. Hell, they used to get dog fighters coming in and asking about their dogs and she'd never freaked out like this.

"Like...not nice."

She rubbed her forehead with the heel of her hand. *Not nice.* That explained everything and nothing all at the same time. "Okay. Stay on this side of the door with your phone ready." She headed toward the front of the small building. "If you hear anything that worries you, call the police."

Emily nodded. "Okay."

Squirting hand sanitizer onto her palm from the bottle on the shelf by the door, she pushed through, giving Emily a reassuring look.

"Hi. How can I…" She froze, ice forming in her veins.

Eddie fucking Perry leaned against the counter as if he had not one fucking care in the world.

An almost overwhelming rush of emotions threatened to break through. Anger. Hatred. Disgust. Even fear as she checked the clock on the wall over his head, making sure K-Squared were still in school.

"Denise. Looking good." His eyes traveled from her head down her body. "No words of welcome for your favorite in-law?" His voice was smooth like honey with just enough of a southern drawl that he didn't sound like a hick. It had always creeped her out how such an evil person could have such an appealing voice.

"No. What do you want Eddie?"

"I want my wife and kids." He said it like he was asking for popcorn and Coke to have during the matinée show at the movie.

"You don't have a wife and kids."

He stood straight and braced his hands on the counter. Emily hadn't been kidding about the tats—he was covered knuckle to neck. He sneered. "I don't care what the courts said, I never signed no divorce papers. Sarah is still my wife and belongs with me."

She inhaled sharply through her nose. Holy shit. He didn't know she was dead. "Yeah, well. Put a bullet in your brain. That's the only way you'll ever get close to Sarah again. Although, you'll be burning in hell, so even that's unlikely."

He slammed his hand down on the counter. "Tell me where the fuck she is!"

His outburst was expected and she didn't flinch. It'd always been his way. Sugary sweet and polite, followed by an violent tantrum when he didn't get his way. Sarah had admitted, after months of therapy, his sweetness had been one of the reasons she'd stay for so long.

"Saint Martin's Episcopal Church. Section four, row twelve, plot three."

"What the fuck does that mean?"

She crossed her arms. "It means she *died*. Ten days ago."

If she hadn't been hyperaware, she might have missed the brief flash of pain that crossed his face. Maybe, in his own sick, demented way, he had loved Sarah. It didn't change anything.

"I want my kids."

Asshole didn't even acknowledge Sarah had died. Didn't ask how or why. He was only worried about what he considered was his.

"You don't have any kids."

"Those kids are mine. They belong with me."

She took a step closer to the counter and the gun she kept in a drop-down compartment underneath. The biometric scanner would recognize her fingerprints and drop the compact nine millimeter into her hand in less than five seconds.

"Your name's not on the birth certificates. You gonna go to court and petition for a DNA test to prove you're the sperm donor?" Maybe she shouldn't taunt him, but she had an over-whelming urge to shoot him and she needed him to take a swing at her first. Wanted fugitive or not, it probably wouldn't be viewed favorably if she shot him just because he was yelling.

His fists clenched and she released her arms, ready to grab her gun. Something crashed in the back. Eddie glanced at the door over her shoulder, then pushed back from the counter.

"It's a nice place you've got here, Denise. Done real good for yourself. That old barn's probably got some really dry wood. Be a shame if something happened to it. No telling what burnt dog smells like." He turned on his heel and pushed through the door.

Fucker. She should have shot him. She pulled her phone out of her pocket.

Emily came in the door behind her. "I called the police when I heard the bang," she said. "I'm sorry I stayed back there."

Denise shot her what she hoped was a reassuring look. "It's alright, Emily."

"Who are you calling?"

She put the phone to her ear. "FBI."

CHAPTER 12

The police were still talking to Emily when Chris arrived with another man. He broke off and joined the two police officers and Emily while Chris approached her.

It was wrong and went against every fiber of her being, but she wanted him to hug her. Take her in his arms, pull her into a tight hug, and tell her everything would be alright. She was not that girl who needed to be coddled and have her problems solved. The thought alone triggered her gag reflex, so what the hell was wrong with her?

He stopped close, his fingers reaching for her face before he seemed to think better of it and he shoved his hands in his pockets. "You okay?"

"Asshole threatened my dogs. No, I'm not okay. I'm pissed the fuck off." She used her residual anger to beat down the softer emotions trying to float to the surface.

A slow smile formed on his lips and a different kind of heat diffused through her body. She hadn't seen him since the morning after the funeral. He'd kissed his way up her back and told her to call him if she needed him for anything. She hadn't until today. Maybe she should have found a reason.

"Well, if nothing else comes this, I think one of the LEOs has a date for this weekend." The guy who'd arrived with Chris broke the spell she'd been falling under.

Spell. Jeez. This was Bree's fault. Her and her damn fairytales.

"Phil Carter. I'm this loser's better half." He cocked his head at Chris and held out his hand. His grip was firm, but not too tight when she shook his hand.

Chris released a long-suffering sigh. "Phil's my partner."

With his receding hairline and slight paunch, indicating muscle gone soft rather than sloth, Phil looked more like a high school football coach than an FBI agent. But who was she to judge?

"Like I said, better half. Before Officer Lothario over there started turning on the charm, I was able to find out you have surveillance cameras?"

Denise looked around Phil to find a blushing Emily handing a phone back to the officer. She watched him hustle back to the patrol car then turned and scuffed her foot on the ground, a big, sappy grin on her face.

There was that gag reflex. "Hot date?" Denise asked.

"He's going to call when he gets off work," Emily said.

"Did you get his number, too?" Phil asked.

Emily shook her head. "No. He had to go so he's going to text me as soon as he can."

Phil wasn't able to hide his look. Denise swallowed a sigh. *Note to self: indoctrinate Emily into the dangers of a player.*

"What?" Emily cast confused looks at all of them.

"I'll explain later," Denise said. "Why don't you call it a day?"

"Are you sure? It's only a little after two."

"Yeah, go on. I'll take care of everything for the afternoon."

Emily played with the end of her braid. "What about...?" She pointed between Chris and Phil.

"I'll answer any questions they have. You already gave a statement to the police. If they have anything else they know where to find you."

"Thanks, Denise." Her phone pinged. She glanced at it and squeed, setting Denise's teeth on edge. "It's him!" She flashed the phone at Denise and went back into reception, thumbs flashing across the screen.

"Huh. He did call. Text. Whatever it is kids do these days," Phil said.

Denise looked at Chris. "Punch your partner, please?"

Chris grinned. "Why don't you punch him?"

"I just met him."

Phil stepped out of striking distance and made a 'T' with his hands. "Time-out. Why am I getting punched? And why wasn't your response, 'because I can't strike a Federal agent?'"

"Well, because I don't have a problem hitting a federal agent."

"True statement." Chris rubbed the corner of his eye, still a little discolored.

Denise gave Chris the stink eye before asking Phil, "And speaking of, you're a federal agent. Where's your poker face?"

"I have three daughters. I gave up poker face a long time ago."

"Yeah...you should work on that a little more. I think you're getting played."

Phil frowned.

"A lot." She did her best to keep a straight face.

Chris coughed into his hand. "Denise. Surveillance."

"Right. I made an extra copy when the cops asked for one. It's in my office." She cocked her head and led them through reception, the small indoor kennel, and to her office in the back corner. Pulling the door open, she kicked the doorstop into place.

"Do you mind if we watch it here?" Chris asked. "That way we can ask questions as we have them."

Denise shrugged. "That's fine." She sat down and logged onto the computer, plugging in the thumb drive she'd saved the video on earlier.

"I'm just saying my girls don't play me a lot," Phil said in a low voice behind her.

"Dude." Chris's voice was full of humor.

Denise smiled at the screen. Any guy who showed that much disappointment for a girl he'd just met was wrapped around the tiny fingers of any daughter he had. Nothing wrong with that as far as she was concerned. Her tough-as-nails father had been the same way with her and Sarah.

She pulled up the video. "I started the recording from the time Eddie pulled into the yard." She felt the two men crowd into the office, close to her back. If she had to guess, Chris was on her right. His scent reminded her of late summer nights.

"How far up the drive is the view from the cameras?" Phil asked.

"Not far. The majority of the cameras focus on the yard between the building and the barn and any access point into the building."

"Why's that?"

She glanced up to her left. "When we first opened we had problems with people trying to steal dogs."

"Seriously?" Chris asked.

Worried her emotions would show on her face if she looked up at him, she looked back to the screen instead. "We're primarily a bully breed rescue. Lots of assholes looking for fighting dogs. That's one reason we decided to start training some of the rescues as service and companion dogs. We could verify a client's need and work with them directly, instead of just adopting a dog out."

On the computer screen a white, four-door sedan pulled into the parking spot nearest the door and Eddie got out of the driver's side.

"Doesn't really seem like his style of car," Denise said.

"It was reported stolen earlier in this morning." Chris's low voice, close to her ear, sent tingles skipping down the side of her neck. He leaned over her shoulder and pointed at the screen. "Can you pause the video?"

It was more of a finger spasm than a controlled click, but she managed to stop the video.

He braced his hand on the desk, surrounding her. "Can't see if there's anyone in the car with him. There's too much reflection on the glass."

Just like when he'd caged her in before, she didn't feel trapped. It should have helped relax her, instead she became hyperaware of his presence next to her and amped up her fight or flight response.

"Did you notice anyone else with him?" Phil asked.

Denise cleared her throat and looked over her shoulder. "He came in by himself. I didn't notice anyone outside waiting for him, but I was focused on not shooting him without justification."

"Good call." Phil's phone rang and he pulled it from the inside pocket of his suit jacket. "Excuse me."

One person leaving her small, cramped office should have relieved some of the tension, but being alone with Chris for the first time since Sarah's funeral just seemed to peg the meter. Flicking her gaze toward him, she asked, "Do you want me to keep playing the video?"

He remained silent and she looked at him fully. His eyes still reminded her of the ocean, blue and clear. She'd always found peace in the ocean.

"Thank you for calling me." His voice was deep and husky— intimate in the small space.

She struggled to control her breathing and keep it even. "It seemed like the right thing to do."

"You could have left it to the cops. They would have called us as soon as they ran his name."

It hadn't crossed her mind. The first person she'd thought to call was him. "I'll do whatever's necessary to protect Kimber and Kaden."

"I know."

He didn't. He had no idea the lengths to which she would go to protect those kids.

His fingers brushed the back of her neck. "We should—"

"They found the car." Phil stopped in the office doorway.

To his credit, Chris didn't jump back like he'd been doing something wrong. Not that he had been. Well…maybe. There was probably some rule against getting involved with a potential witness in a federal investigation. Were they involved? Did she want to be involved? Was that even something she was capable of at this point?

Phil's gaze moved between them before settling on Chris. "Local LEOs have a forensics team on site, but the Chief wants us to check it out before they tow the car."

Chris rose from his lean over her shoulder. "Sure."

Denise closed the program and pulled out the thumb drive, holding it out to Chris. What had he been about to say? They should talk? Probably, but she had not one idea about what she would say.

"Thanks." He took the drive from her and gestured to the door. "Are you staying here?"

"No." She wheeled the chair back from the desk and stood. "I need to take some of the dogs out and I still have a few training sessions this afternoon."

"By yourself?" Chris asked.

"I don't think that's a good idea," Phil said. "You shouldn't be here alone. Just because they found the car doesn't mean he won't come back."

Her eyes rolled so hard she worried she may have given herself a headache. "I texted my other part-timer and asked him to come in. Mostly because I need the help, otherwise I'll be here all night." She shooed Phil out of the doorway. "I've also got two possible adoption appointments coming by around four." She led the way through the row of kennels. "And I'm armed now."

"Is this the dog we picked up?"

Almost to the top of the row, she stopped and turned to see Chris in front of Sweetpea's cage. The small dog's butt looked like it had a live wire attached to it given how fast it wiggled back and forth. She joined the two men in front of the cage. "Yeah."

"Is she still up for adoption?" Chris unlatched the gate and swung it open, crouching in the opening. The dog launched herself at him and tried to bathe his face with her tongue.

Hmm…how to answer that question. "She was. I decided Kimber and Kaden needed a dog, so I'm going to keep her."

"Really? What about her puppies?" He rubbed the dog's cheeks, but looked up at Denise.

"They were all adopted out, almost as soon as they were weaned."

"That's too bad." A final pat on her side and he pushed the dog back into the kennel. "I've been thinking I need some company at home." He rose and closed the gate, dropping the latch into place.

"How many of these dogs are up for adoption?" Phil asked.

Denise fell in beside them as they continued to the front entrance. "All the dogs in here, except Sweetpea, are boarders or here for training." They walked through the reception area and out the front door.

"What about in the barn?"

"Fourteen dogs in the barn, three of which are being assessed for the K9 program."

"Wow," Phil said. "And you manage all this by yourself?"

She shrugged. "I have the two part-time employees, plus several volunteers who come out a few days a week."

He stopped in front of their dark blue sedan. "Still, that's a lot for one person."

"It's a full-time job. I don't imagine the FBI is an eight-to-four gig."

Phil huffed out a laugh. "No. No, it's not." He held out his hand. "Thank you for your help."

She shook his hand. "You're welcome, but if he comes back, it'll be me needing your help."

"Let's hope it doesn't come to that." He walked around the hood and got in the driver's side.

Chris's hand landed on the small of her back when he stepped around her. "I'll call you later?"

She hesitated briefly, then nodded. Whether she'd be ready to talk to him when he called was a completely different matter.

"Be safe." The slight rise of his voice at the end softened his command. He squeezed her hip and got in the passenger side.

Waiting until they reached the top of the drive, she checked the time and jogged up the stairs to her apartment. Going directly to her side of the bed, she knelt down and reached between the slat and the box spring, pulling the small flip phone from its hiding spot. Opening it, she powered it on. Twenty-three percent battery was all she needed and she dialed the number from memory.

Four rings and it connected. "I need a favor," she said without waiting for a "hello."

"Pretty big favor if you're calling me."

Like she'd told Chris, she'd do whatever it took to protect her kids. "Graham."

"What do you need?"

"Can you meet?"

~

SHE'D CHOSEN a small table in the back corner of Panera after ordering a latte. They'd both be able to sit with their backs to the wall and still view the exits. Sprocket lay at her feet, content for the moment, but Denise had seen her eyeing the display case.

A tall, well-built man with a salt-and-pepper beard entered through the side door and beelined for her. It took her several seconds to reconcile the attractive man in front of her with her former OIC. Not that he hadn't been good-looking a decade ago, but he'd been leaner. And the hair had been on top of his head instead of his face.

He sat in the chair directly facing the restaurant, as she'd expected him to. "Sorry to hear about Sarah."

Nodding, she sipped her latte. It was still too raw to acknowledge the condolences without the sting of tears pricking her nose and the backs of her eyes.

"I had my people look into her ex, but I need to know what you want specifically."

She'd always appreciated his direct, no bullshit style. "I need someone on the kids."

He threaded his fingers together on the table. "The FBI doesn't have a trail on them?"

"Not that I'm aware of."

"And if you were aware of it?"

How to frame her response? "I wouldn't trust they'd put the safety and well-being of my kids ahead of the target."

He raised his eyebrows. "Even the guy you're dating?"

"We're not dating," she said quickly. Maybe too quickly, judging by Graham's continued questioning look. She sighed. "He has to operate under certain legal constraints. You have a lot more flexibility."

"What do you want me to do with any information on the ex's activities."

"Can you feed it anonymously to the FBI?" she asked.

"If that's what you want, yes."

She nodded. "The sooner this is over the better."

"Do you want us on your house and the rescue?"

"Only as far as keeping an eye on Kaden and Kimber."

His steely gray eyes assessed her. "You know the job offer still stands."

She shook her head. He'd offered her a job when he'd started his private security company five years ago. She hadn't been in a position to accept then and she had no desire to accept his offer now. "I like where I am."

"But are you happy?" he asked.

It wasn't a question she'd really ever considered. "Sometimes it's not about being happy. Sometimes it's about being content."

"That's a shitty way to live your life."

"Are you happy?" she asked.

Something dark and pained crossed his face, there and gone in a blink. He rapped the table with his knuckles. "We'll keep them safe. Call if you need anything else."

CHAPTER 13

"*I*'m going to buy the kids a play set for the backyard."
Bree upended the wine bottle, pouring the last of it
into her glass.

"What kind of play set?" Denise asked. But the answer was
delayed by the ripping sound of packing tape as Denise closed the
box she'd finished stuffing full of books and movies.

"A wooden one with a slide and swing." Bree leaned against the
counter and sipped her wine.

She wasn't fooled by that innocent look, envisioning a
massive, Swiss Family Robinson monstrosity taking up the entire
yard of Bree's house. She set her hands on her hips. "Show me."

Bree rolled her eyes. "It's not that big."

"Show. Me."

Setting down her wine glass with a sign, she pulled out her
phone, fiddled with it, and handed it over to Denise

Her estimation hadn't been far off. The damn thing had a
turret. "No." She handed the phone back to Bree. "It's too big and
too expensive."

"It's not and it's awesome. *I* want to play in it."

"It is and you can—in something smaller and less expensive."

"But look, with this one you can hook up a hose and shoot the water cannon." She held out the phone, zoomed in on the picture of a boy shooting a water cannon from the top of the tower.

Denise set up another box. "Uh huh. Are you buying this for them or you?"

Bree slid her phone back into her pocket. "We'll call it a mutually beneficial purchase."

"Get a smaller one."

Bree's shoulders sagged and she picked up her wine glass. "Fine."

"You're going to get that one, aren't you?"

She flashed Denise a shit-eating grin. "Yup."

Denise growled in frustration. "You can get it for them for Christmas."

"But that's months away."

"And it doubles as their birthday present as well." She held her friend's gaze, knowing she wouldn't win the argument about the Fort Knox of play sets, but unwilling to give on the when or why.

Bree broke the stare-down. "Fine," she said in defeat.

Denise dropped a stack of DVDs in the box. "I thought you were going to help me pack."

"I am. I'm helping you get rid of the stuff you don't want to move."

She looked up sharply. "Did you drink the last of my wine?"

"You still have two more bottles."

"Phew," Denise said. "I thought I was going to have to kick you out. Pour me a glass, would you?"

"Sure." Bree took a glass down from the cupboard and uncorked a bottle. "Besides...I thought you were finally going to tell me what happened between you and Chris the night of Sarah's funeral."

Denise fumbled the DVD cases, sending them crashing to the

96

ground. Shooting Bree a baleful look, she stooped to pick them up. "Who said anything happened?"

"You didn't say nothing happened, so process of elimination says something happened."

Avoiding her intense and all-too-knowing gaze, Denise flipped the cases so they all faced the same way. Something happened alright. Something was still happening. Or could happen, if she gave it a chance.

She shoved the stack of movies in the box. "I lost my shit, we had sex, and I cried." Bree wasn't going to be satisfied with that answer, but she deserved a little bit of shock factor.

"You...what?" Bree set the wine bottle down with a thud.

"You look like a fish. Close your mouth."

"I'm not a guppy."

"What?"

"Nothing. Go back and start at the beginning."

Denise hid her grin. "Hang on." She needed to make sure there were no little ears listening.

Down the hall, Kimber and Kaden sat on Kimber's bed watching a show on their tablet, Sprocket taking up the entire foot of the bed. "You guys okay?" she asked from the doorway.

All three looked up. "Yes," Kimber said.

"Thirty minutes, then teeth and stories."

"Okay, Aunt Denny." The kids went back to staring at the tablet and Sprocket laid her head back on her paws.

They seemed to be holding it together, but it was hard to tell. They had their first session with the grief counselor in a couple of days. The truth would come out eventually. Until then, she wouldn't push them, knowing from experience how much it could backfire.

Heading back to the main part of the house, she picked up the wine glass and sat opposite Bree on the couch.

"They good?"

"They appear to be. We'll see after next week."

Bree nodded. "Spill. Losing your shit, sex, crying. You don't have to go in that order. In fact, start with the sex." She wagged her eyebrows.

Denise sipped her wine, a flush that had nothing to do with the pinot grigio blooming high on her cheeks. "It was...good. Better than good. Until I started crying and tried to kick him out."

Two slow blinks. "Tried. Maybe you should start with losing your shit."

Staring down at her glass, she thought back to that moment. "I broke. I hit the wall and I hit it hard. Everything just... I couldn't keep it locked down anymore."

"Finally," Bree said.

Denise snapped her head up at her friend's sigh of relief. "What do you mean 'finally?'"

"You know you're my favorite person, but, dude, I've been waiting for it for weeks. Months, honestly. Ever since Sarah was diagnosed."

"Why didn't you say anything?"

Bree cocked her head to the side. "Because I know you. If I had asked you'd have told me everything was fine. And the few times I did ask, that's exactly what you did. I figured that night was going to be the breaking point. That's why I sent Chris after you."

God, she loved Bree. Loved that she understood her and all her fucked-up-ness. "I wondered."

"You needed a target. Someone you could unload on and not feel guilty about doing it. That wasn't me or your parents."

"No. It wasn't. I didn't need to be coddled and I didn't want to burden anyone when I lost it."

Bree scooted closer on the couch so their knees were almost touching. "You have to stop doing that. You're not a burden. You don't always have to be the strong one that holds everyone else together. You suck up everyone else's problems until there's no room left for your own and then you lose your shit."

"I know. You're right."

"Of course I am."

Denise smiled, even though the backs of her eyes pricked. Even now, with the person she felt safest with, she tried to hold back.

"Promise me you'll talk to me before you get to that point again."

She licked her lips. "I'll try."

Bree nodded. "So that's losing your shit. Sex?"

"I'm flattered, but no."

"Ha. Ha." She smacked Denise's knee. "Don't be a dick. Besides, I'm getting it good at home."

"No. No. And more no. I already know too much as it is about you and Jase. I have a hard enough time looking him in the eyes, I don't need more details."

"Yeah, well. I don't have that problem." She drained her glass and went to the kitchen counter, bringing the bottle back with her. "The only reason I haven't asked Chris to show me his signature move is because I'm still in the 'we're angry at Chris' camp." She sat back on the couch. "Unless we're not?"

"I can't believe I told you that story." Denise took the wine bottle and topped off her glass, then set it on the coffee table. "We're not, but I'm pretty sure Jase would not like you asking Chris to strip for you."

"Hmm…good point. Anyway. You? Chris? Sex?"

She took a fortifying sip. "I attacked him when he found me."

Bree's forehead wrinkled. "Physically or sexually?"

"Both."

"Uh, which did you do first?"

"Physical. Then the other one."

"And you had sex?"

She half nodded. "And we…had sex." Why was it so hard to share this with Bree? She's shared before. The strip show. The kiss in the woods. Eventually, over shots of Jameson, she'd shared the rest of it. Sharing the details of this felt different for some reason.

"But it was…more…than just sex," Bree hedged.

"It was…more."

"Oh my God!" Bree dropped her head back and stared at the ceiling. "Getting information out of you is like popping a zit."

Denise's nose wrinkled. "Ew. What?"

She raised her head. "It's like popping a zit that's not quite ready, but you know if you work at it a little, maybe poke it with a needle to get it started, it's going to explode everywhere."

Her best friend had compared her to a zit. "I am equal parts offended and disgusted."

"Be the zit, Denise. You'll feel better once the nasty center is purged and the pressure is relieved."

"You're ridiculous. And did I mention disgusting? Fine! It started as fucking and he ended up making love to me. He made me look in his eyes and it was deep and meaningful and it freaked me the fuck out. Happy now?"

"Fuck yes!" The damn woman pumped her fist in the air. "And?"

"And I started crying, pushed him off me, and told him to leave."

Bree's shoulders slumped. "Denise."

She averted her gaze and took a large swallow of her wine. It hadn't been her finest moment, especially given her general "I-am-woman-fuck-your-expectations" persona.

"Did he?" Bree asked.

"No. He picked me up, put me in bed, and spooned me."

Two seconds later Bree threw back her head, laughing. "You have got to be the only woman in the history of women to be disgruntled that a hot guy spooned her after making love to her."

Her lips twitched. It was a little funny. "Whatever. I hate you."

Bree laughed for several moments before sighing and wiping under an eye.

"I told him about Ali," Denise said quietly.

That statement killed her humor. "Holy shit. Really?"

"Yeah."

"Wow. That's… You like him."

Denise pulled her lips between her teeth.

"You like him, like him. Like…don't want to talk about it because if you do, you'll jinx it, like him." Bree's voice was filled with shock and wonder.

"Don't be so surprised," Denise said. Maybe that was it. If she gave words to what she was feeling, it ran the risk of turning to shit. If she ignored it, it'd be like it never happened.

"How'd you leave it? You know, after?"

"He kissed me goodbye and told me to call him if I needed anything."

"Did you call him?" she asked.

"No. Not until today."

"Why not?"

She closed her eyes, trying to verbalize all the roadblocks to moving forward. "Because last time, he ghosted."

"But—"

"I understand it was his job." Denise opened her eyes. "He explained and he apologized, but I can't help but wonder if he would have contacted me if I hadn't been here that day he came looking for Sarah. I also can't help wondering how much of him being around is him needing me and the kids to get to Eddie."

"Chris doesn't strike me as the kind of guy to use kids to further his agenda."

She picked at the skin around her thumbnail. "I want to believe that as well."

"But you don't."

Deep down she did. As unfair as it was to compare Chris to what had happened in the past, there was too much at stake. "I struggle with it."

"Do you remember what you said to me when I was having doubts about Jase?" Bree asked.

Denise pursed her lips and sipped her wine. "I'm sure it was something sage and wise and nothing I want repeated back to me."

"Too bad. You told me to give it a chance. That some things are worth fighting for."

"Yeah, well. Those who can't do, impart words of wisdom."

Bree rolled her eyes. "You can do and you should. If Eddie and Chris's job weren't a factor, would you want to give it a shot?"

Would she? He was smart and funny and sexy as hell. He appeared to appreciate her sarcasm. She felt more like her, the old her, than she had in years when he was around. The tiny ember of hope she kept locked up tight flared to life around him, as if he were a drop of fuel on a dying fire. Just enough for it to feed the flames and burn away the darkness.

"Yes." She wanted to give it—them—a chance.

"Then give it a shot."

"Just that easy?" She remembered what she'd said to Bree.

So did Bree. "Nothing worth fighting for is ever easy."

But could it be? Maybe once they got through the situation with Eddie. "There's more."

"Well, it's too early to know you're pregnant, so it can't be that."

"Sweet baby—" She covered her eyes. "Why would you even put that out in the universe?"

"Just saying."

Denise dropped her hand. "Eddie made an appearance at the rescue today."

"What the fuck? You didn't lead with that?"

"You were the one who wanted all the dirty details about my sex life."

Bree shook her head. "Whatever." She leaned forward. "Where did you stash the body?" she whispered.

Denise closed the gap. "I didn't kill him."

"Why not?" she asked in a normal voice.

Denise leaned back. "Video cameras and witnesses for one. For another, it's kind of hard to be K-Squared's guardian if I'm in jail."

A tiny growl of frustration escaped Bree as she leaned back against the armrest of the couch.

Denise recounted Eddie's appearance and threats, as well as the need for more cameras around the barn.

"Make the call tomorrow. Ask them to do a rush install." She rubbed a finger across her bottom lip. "You know who you should call?"

Denise nodded. "I already called him."

Bree's eyebrows shot up. "You did?"

"Nobody's getting near my kids, Bree. Even if it means I have to call in a favor from Graham."

"Got it."

Denise checked her watch. "Why don't you go say goodnight to them? It's been way more than thirty minutes and it's a school night."

Bree grinned. "Who'd've thought you'd be worried about school nights?"

"Sure as hell wasn't me."

She gathered up the wine glasses and empty bottle while Bree said goodbye to K-Squared. She smiled at the giggles she could hear coming from their room. They'd always loved Bree. Sarah had been right. This was the best thing for Kaden and Kimber. She still worried she was going to screw them up. Lord knew she'd never be a PTA mom. But between her parents and Bree and Gran, she'd figure it out.

Bree came from their room, grinning. "I got them all riled up for you."

"Awesome, thanks for that."

"You're welcome." She grabbed her wallet and keys from the

bookcase by the door. "You realize I'm Team Chris from this point forward, right?"

"Yeah. Kind of worked that one out."

"Unless he screws up again. Then I'm totally back on Team Denise and we'll figure out the alibis later."

CHAPTER 14

*C*hris reclined the driver's seat back a few more inches. He'd been sitting in his truck for almost three hours. Bree's car had been in the drive when he arrived, so he'd parked a few houses down to avoid her spotting his truck. Denise had walked her to the door thirty minutes ago and a few lights had gone off.

Glancing down at this phone, he dimmed the brightness and opened his ebook app. Rereading *Pet Sematary* would keep him awake, even if it made him damn glad he didn't own a cat.

The phone rang, Denise's name appearing on the screen. "Hey."

"Hey." She didn't say anything else.

"Everything okay?" He looked up the street toward her house.

"I'm not sure."

He sat up straight and scanned around the house for anything unusual. "What do you mean?"

"I think I should call the cops."

He couldn't see anything from where he was parked. Was something going on at the back of the house? He thumbed the control to raise the back of his seat. "What's going on?"

"I think there's a creeper parked down the street."

He paused with his hand on the ignition button. "A what?"

"You know…a creeper. Stalker. Weirdo."

He relaxed back into his seat. "Why does it have to be a weirdo?" Guaranteed she'd spotted him and was fucking with him.

"Well, he keeps shifting around in his seat like he's rubbing one out."

"I'm—" A knock on the passenger-side window interrupted him. Sighing, he ended the call and unlocked the doors.

Denise climbed inside and pulled the door shut. "Whatcha doin'?"

"*Not* rubbing one out."

"So I can see." She glanced down at his lap.

Was that disappointment he heard? His dick stirred to life, taking a sudden interest in the idea of her watching him stroke himself. He had a hard time, no pun intended, reconciling her flirtiness with the silent treatment he'd received the last couple of weeks.

"When did you spot me?"

"The second or third time you drove by looking for a spot to park." She leaned against the door and angled her body toward him. "So is this sanctioned surveillance or are you here on your own time?"

"Not sanctioned. Yet," he emphasized. The paperwork was in, but the higher-ups didn't see the need to put someone on her and the kids twenty-four, seven at the moment.

She nodded. "That's what I figured. So what's the goal? Protection or catch Eddie and any of his accomplices?"

"Protection." Not one fucking thing was going to happen to her or her kids. His gut still churned thinking about what could have happened at the rescue today. There was no telling what Eddie was capable of and he hated not being able to help Denise. No, she didn't exactly need it, but that didn't matter to him. Call him a Neanderthal, but he wanted to make sure she was safe. Catching Eddie was secondary.

"Why don't you pull into the drive then? You can provide protection from inside just as well as outside."

His little brain heard *protection* and *inside* and was all for the idea. His big brain knew he'd be as useful as kitten mittens if he was anywhere near Denise and a bed.

"I don't know if that's the best idea." He shifted his arm, trying to surreptitiously cover his growing erection.

Her gaze dropped to his lap again. "If you stay, you'll be staying on the couch. And you'll be leaving before I wake up the kids for school. I don't want them getting the wrong idea or asking any uncomfortable questions."

What was the wrong idea?

"Besides, I need help packing. All Bree did was drink my wine and talk me into letting her buy a huge-ass play set for the kids."

She pointed to her house and he begrudgingly started his truck. Checking the side mirror, he pulled into the road then her short drive.

Shutting off the engine, he set the parking brake. "You don't want them to have a play set?"

"It's not that. The one she wants to get is a couple grand and will take up half the yard. Plus, I know she's taking a lot less in rent than what she can get for the house."

She hopped down from the truck and eased the door shut so it didn't slam. He did the same and rounded the front end.

"Is she getting them a play set?" Stealing the opportunity touch her, he rested his palm on the small of her back as she led the way to the door. Walking behind her, he couldn't help but appreciate the way her leggings hugged her hips and showed off her legs.

"I told her she could get it for them as a combined birthday and Christmas present." She pushed through the door and kicked her shoes off onto the small stand behind it. She waited for him to clear the threshold, then closed the door and threw the deadbolt.

He added his shoes to the pile and followed her toward the kitchen, sitting on the stool he'd occupied during the wake. The house seemed much larger now that there weren't a few dozen people crammed into it.

"You want something to drink?" she asked.

"Water's fine. How close are their birthdays?"

She opened the fridge she'd just closed and pulled out two beers, closing the door with her hip. "I'm going to need more than water if we're going to talk about this."

"Okay…" He wasn't sure what *this* was or why he was going to need a beer to hear it.

Her gaze moved behind him, to where he knew the kids' bedroom was. "They asleep?"

"Yeah." She twisted off the top and took a pull from the bottle, her soft lips pursing around the opening. The label caught his eye. It was the same microbrew he'd brought to her house the first time they'd had sex and he pressed his lips together to keep from smiling.

Setting the bottle on the counter, she took a deep breath. "They're eleven months apart. Their birthdays are March and February."

"You called them Irish twins."

She nodded. "Eddie raped Sarah three weeks after she'd given birth to Kaden. She found out she was pregnant at her six-week postpartum checkup. He started beating her in the car on the way home, blaming her for another mouth to feed. When he stopped for gas, the guy on the other side of the pump saw Sarah and asked if she needed help and offered to call the police." She finally looked up from the counter. "Eddie beat him to death."

"Fuck." *The Good Samaritan.* He twisted off the cap of his beer and took a long swallow.

"He was twenty-eight, he was engaged, and he was on his way to get fitted for his tux for his wedding."

Taking another swallow, he tried not to gag as it trickled past the knot in his throat.

"I was in Iraq when it happened. Sarah was hospitalized for a week and I went home on emergency leave."

All the pieces fell into place. "That's when that boy —Ali—died."

Her eyelashes lowered, hiding her eyes and nodded.

"Denise." He couldn't form any words. What did he even begin to say to something like that?

"To the FBI, Eddie's just another criminal. A small cog in a bigger piece of machinery you're trying to stop." She looked back at him, her eyes ablaze with fury and unshed tears. "But to me? He's the piece of shit that almost took my family from me and is trying to again. I'd as soon shoot him as look at him, but I can't because it's not just me I have to worry about anymore."

Her hands fisted on the counter. "I promised myself I would never be helpless again. That I would never be in a position where a child's life was threatened. So tell me what the fuck I'm supposed to do now."

He covered her fists with his hands and used his thumbs to rub the meaty pad of her palm until her hands relaxed. "You trust me to help you. You trust me to do the right thing for you and Kimber and Kaden."

He held her gaze, silently pleading with her to take the help he was offering. He wasn't lying. He would do the right thing to protect her, even if the right thing didn't fall in line with the FBI's agenda.

She nodded tightly and a wave of relief washed over him. He'd never do anything to make her regret her decision. To make her regret giving him a second chance.

CHAPTER 15

*H*e was being stared at. And not in the soft and sultry way he wanted Denise to stare at him while she mentally undressed him. Or physically—he wasn't picky. This stare was hard and suspicious.

Cracking open an eyelid, he found Kaden sitting on the coffee table. Opening both eyes fully, he angled his head on the pillow Denise had left him and rubbed his eyes. "Good morning."

"Why are you asleep on our couch?"

Shit. The last thing he expected to wake up to was an interrogation. Denise was supposed to have woken him before she got the kids up so he could leave without them seeing him.

"Uh. I was helping your aunt pack last night and it got really late. I was too tired to drive home, so she let me sleep on the couch."

"Aunt Denny's still asleep." Kaden at with his hands tucked between his knees as if he expected Chris to have a solution to the problem.

He checked his watch and sat up fully, swinging his feet to the floor. "What time do you have to catch the bus? Do you take the bus or does Denise take you?"

"We take the bus. Aunt Denny walks us to the bus stop at seven-thirty. No one else's parents walk them to the bus stop. Aunt Denny said it's because those parents don't like their kids as much as she likes us. I don't know if that's true. Except for maybe Justice. He's a bully. He tries to take everyone's toys if they bring one to school. He tried to pull Kimber's hair one day, but I told him I'd punch him in the ball sac if he did it. My mom said it was my job to protect her because all little girls deserve protection. Except when she plays with my Power Rangers and makes them marry her Barbie. Then I don't want to protect her."

Holy word vomit. Did all little kids talk that much? He scrubbed a hand over his head. "Uh, I don't know how much other parents like their kids, but I know Denise likes you and your sister a whole lot. Why don't we let her sleep for a few more minutes and I'll help you with breakfast?"

Kaden gazed at him somberly, as if weighing the pros and cons of his decision. "Okay."

Chris smiled. "Okay. Is Kimber awake?"

"Not yet."

"Why don't you wake her up and get dressed and I'll fix your breakfast. What do you normally have?"

"Scrambled eggs and toast with peanut butter and milk."

Chris nodded and found a whole new level of respect for what Denise had to handle since she'd taken on the care of Kaden and Kimber. "I should be able to figure that out. You got your part covered?"

Kaden nodded back.

"Let's do it." He held his fist up for a bump. Kaden stared at it, stared at Chris, then back at his fist. For one awkward moment, he thought the little boy would leave him hanging. He didn't think his ego would take being dissed by a nine-year-old, but Kaden finally bumped his fist with his own.

Pride swelled in his chest like he'd been given a special, once-in-a-lifetime gift. Hell, maybe he had been. Kaden stood and shuffled down the hall. Chris scratched at the stubble on his chin. His whole existence had just been validated by a fist bump from a kid. Shaking his head, he pushed to his feet and checked on Denise.

She'd left the door to her room cracked, probably so she could hear the kids if they woke up during the night. Pushing it open a little more, he found her sprawled on her stomach, wrapped around a pillow with her hair spread out behind her. He could see the sweet spot next to her where he'd fit perfectly—his face tucked into the curve of her neck, arm thrown over her, his leg nestled between hers.

Sprocket raised her head from her position at the end of the bed and regarded him with her large brown eyes.

Great. Now he was being judged by a dog.

Easing the door closed, he went into the small galley kitchen. Opening and closing the few lower cabinets, he found a skillet for the eggs. Kaden and Kimber climbed onto the stools at the small eat-at counter that formed an "L" on one side of the kitchen while he pulled eggs and milk from the fridge.

Setting the ingredients on the counter, he braced his hands on the edge. "Let's talk eggs. Hard or soft?"

Kimber rubbed her eyes and yawned. "Huh?"

"Do you like them a little runny or cooked really well?"

"Really well," Kaden said.

"Runny eggs are gross," Kimber added.

"Runny equals gross. Got it." Chris nodded and opened more cupboards until he found a bowl. Pulling a fork from the drawer in front of him, he scrambled eggs under the intense scrutiny of two kids. He couldn't remember the last time he'd been in such a nerve-wracking situation—not even when he'd been going through evaluation at the FBI Academy.

They whispered to themselves while he stirred the eggs. He made eggs almost every morning, but this morning he felt like he was auditioning for a cooking show, presenting his creation to the top foodies in the country. Maybe they were the Gordon

Ramsay of second and third grade and they were critiquing his technique.

"Where can I find plates?" he asked, turning the burner off and moving the skillet over.

"Our plates are in the big bottom drawer," Kaden said.

"You have your own plates?"

"Mine's the purple one," Kimber said.

Sure enough, a stack of plastic colored plates and utensils took up the bottom drawer. Still hunched over, he asked, "Kaden, what color do you want?"

"Orange."

Chris pulled out the requested plates and matching forks. When he rose from his crouch, Kimber was whispering in Kaden's ear. "What's up? Are these the wrong plates?"

Kaden shook his head. "No. She wants to know if you're going to do her hair for school."

He...what? No. He was not trained for that. "Uh, I think we'll wake your aunt up to do that. I would probably make a horrible mess of it." There was no probably about it. Even the idea of trying to figure out what he was supposed to do with Kimber's waist-long hair had him longing to be hunkered down behind a makeshift barrier taking fire from an unseen enemy. Taliban ambush in the wilds of Afghanistan? Bring it on. Fixing a little girl's hair? No, sir-ee.

A muffled "shit" followed closely by a bark from Sprocket derailed his thought train.

"Looks like Denise is awake."

Kimber giggled behind her hand and he winked at the little girl. Taking the pan from the stove, he divided the eggs between the two plates. He set the pan on the stove and popped bread into the toaster.

"Kaden! Kimber! Wake up, guys. We're late." Denise rushed out of her room and across the small living room, dining room combo, pulling her hair up into a messy bun on her head.

Long hair was absolutely her territory. No one said anything as she went down the short hallway. Kimber giggled quietly and Kaden smiled before taking a bite of eggs. It was like they were all part of an inside joke, none of them willing to be the first one to call attention to themselves in the kitchen. Inexplicable warmth spread through Chris's chest.

Shit. He had no business feeling this comfortable with these kids.

"Kaden? Kimber? Where—?" She stopped in the living room, hands her hips, having finally spotted them.

Kaden laughed and Kimber giggled again. Denise smiled, thankfully. "What are you guys doing?" she asked.

"Eating breakfast, silly," Kimber said.

"I see that. Did you guys make that or did Mr. Chris make it for you?" Her eyebrows rose in question.

Shit. He might have made a huge error in judgment. He looked at it from Denise's point of view and realized he should have woken her up as soon as Kaden went to get Kimber. He'd only been trying to do something nice for Denise by letting her sleep a few more minutes, but now he thought she might look at it as him trying to manipulate the kids.

Fuck.

"Mr. Chris made eggs," Kaden said. "We were going to wake you up to do Kimber's hair. He looked a little freaked out when she asked if he was going to do it for her."

"He did, huh?" She joined them in the kitchen. "Don't suppose he made coffee too, did he?"

He couldn't tell if she was pissed that he'd overstepped his bounds. "No, unfortunately I haven't gotten around to that."

She grabbed the carafe from the coffee maker, filling it with water from the sink. She quickly set the coffee up to brew. "You guys good with buying lunch today or do you want me to make you something real quick?"

"Can I take my lunch?" Kimber asked. "I don't like the stuff they give us at school. It's always mushy."

"Yeah, baby. I'll make you lunch." She pulled down a jar of peanut butter and held it out to Chris.

"What's this for?"

"Toast." She pointed behind him.

The bread had popped up while he'd been assessing her level of anger. He took the jar and grabbed a knife from the drawer. She didn't appear to be angry at all. Either that, or she was hiding it well. Given he'd never been able to read her under normal circumstances, he'd probably have to wait until the kids were on the bus before she unloaded on him.

He set the toast on the kids' plates and moved out of the kitchen. Leaning against the counter across from the kids, he watched Denise prepare their lunches. She seemed to do every-thing at once—taking coffee mugs down, pulling out fruit and vegetables, bread and lunch meat, sandwich bags and lunch containers. In less time than it took for him to find their colored plates, she had their lunches packed and ready to go.

"Okay, guys. Plates in the sink, then brush your teeth. We've got to hurry or you'll miss the bus."

"Aunt Denny, will you braid my hair today?" Kimber asked.

"Sure. Bring me your brush when you're done brushing your teeth."

"Okay." The kids hopped down from the stools and dropped their plates in the sink, before running to the bathroom.

Chris wasn't sure if he should offer to help with something else or stay out of the way of their routine. He gathered up the remaining dirty dishes from breakfast and set them in the sink, running water over them so the food wouldn't stick.

"You can leave those, I'll wash them later."

"It's no problem," he said.

She didn't say anything as Kimber returned with a brush and some hair clips. She climbed back up on the stool and folded her hands on the counter while Denise brushed out her hair. Denise's nimble fingers gathered up sections of Kimber's hair and quickly had it braided down her back. After securing the end, she clipped barrettes into the sides.

"There you go. Shoes on. Jacket on. Get your backpack. Kaden! Let's go, buddy."

"I'm ready, Aunt Denny."

Denise herded them toward the door, slipping into flip-flops, pulling a hoodie over her head, and grabbing her keys as she ushered the kids outside.

The silence when they left was deafening after the commotion of the last few minutes. He stared down at Sprocket, curled up on a dog bed in the corner of the dining room. "Am I supposed to wait for her or am I supposed to leave."

The dog licked her chops, whined, and rolled to her side.

"Thanks. That clears that up."

CHAPTER 16

"*I* like Mr. Chris," Kimber said.

Denise looked down at her. "You do?"

"Uh huh." She swung their hands as they walked.

"What do you like about him?"

"He makes good eggs."

She smiled at the simplicity of Kimber's statement. If only the rest of life was as simple as whether or not someone could scramble eggs.

"Did he ask you guys any questions?"

"Yes," Kaden said.

Her stomach dropped and she worked to control her initial reaction. She hadn't expected the answer to be yes. Had he used her oversleeping as an opportunity to get information from the kids? "What kinds of questions?"

"How we like our eggs," Kaden said.

The sense of relief was instant and almost euphoric and she hated that for one short instant she'd doubted his intentions, but old habits died hard. Expect the worst and you won't ever be disappointed. Funny...she'd still been disappointed when she'd thought the worst.

"He had to ask where our plates were," Kimber added. "And he didn't want to do my hair."

The image of Chris trying to braid Kimber's hair flashed through her mind. A small, hard knot in her chest unfurled at the picture it created. She mentally shoved the whole idea back into its metaphysical corner.

"Is he your boyfriend?" Kaden asked.

Denise coughed, choking on the spit that found its way down the wrong pipe with her surprise. "Why would you ask that?"

"'Cause he was asleep on the couch."

"No. He's not my boyfriend." Truthfully, she didn't know how to describe Chris. They'd had something a few months ago that could have been more. They had...something...now, but she had no idea what it was or how to categorize it. All of which was too complicated to tell a nine- and eight-year-old.

"He's just a friend."

"Oh," Kimber said with a good deal of disappointment.

"Why do you say it like that?" Denise asked.

"Amber's mom has a boyfriend and he takes them to dinner and movies sometimes."

"Do you want to go to dinner and movies sometimes?" Of course they did. Damn, she hadn't really done anything fun with them, had she? They'd been so focused on getting through Sarah's cancer, she completely forgot they were just kids and needed to do fun things.

"Tell you what—how about tomorrow, I pick you up from school and we go see a movie and then go someplace fun for dinner?"

"Chuck E. Cheese?" Kimber's eyes lit up with delight.

The corner of Denise's eye twitched at the thought. "We'll see about that. I don't know if they would allow Sprocket in there with us and I'd need to take her to a place like that."

"Oh, yeah," Kaden said. He looked around Denise as they stood waiting for the bus. "Kimber, Mom said loud noises and stuff like

120

that bother Aunt Denny, remember? We should pick something else."

"It's okay, Aunt Denny. We don't have to go there," Kimber said.

Great. Now her PTSD was affecting them. Awesome. She knelt down so she was eye-level with Kimber. "Sweetie, it's not your job to worry about me. I love that you care enough to be willing to give up something you want to do because you know it will make me uncomfortable, but I'm the grown-up. I'll figure something out so we can do something fun, okay?"

"But I love you, Aunt Denny. I don't want you to be upset."

Kimber completely wrecked her. Took a hammer and smashed up her hardened heart until all that was left was the soft, vulnerable, defenseless center. The bus pulled up at the corner and the doors opened with a low squeak. She glanced over at the kids lining up to get on. "I love you too, baby. We'll figure it out, okay?"

"Okay." Kimber threw her arms around her neck. "Love you."

Kaden kissed her cheek quickly and ran for the bus, as if he were afraid his friends might see him being affectionate. Denise smiled and stood, watching until the bus pulled away from the curb and was out of sight.

Heading back to the house, realization struck. She loved them, but it had always been in the way that she loved all her family—unconditionally and unquestioning. It simply was.

While she knew her family loved her in return, until that moment she didn't realize the depth of love a child could provide. Realizing Kimber loved her enough to unselfishly sacrifice her own desires, at eight years old, tilted the axis of her world.

She'd said she'd do anything to protect them—and she would, without a second's hesitation—but until then even she hadn't understood to what lengths she would go to do that. There were none. No line she wouldn't cross.

It terrified her. Not that they loved her or that she loved them, but if anything were to happen to them, she knew she wouldn't survive the devastation.

She pushed through the front door and closed it behind her, throwing the dead bolt. Sprocket trotted over to her and pawed at her knees. Kneeling down, she buried her face in her dog's neck, wrapping her arms around her. Sprocket rested her head on Denise's shoulder, giving her the comfort she needed.

"Everything okay?"

Opening her eyes, she found Chris standing in the small dining room, his eyes filled with concern. Shit. She'd been in such a daze it hadn't even registered his truck was still parked in the drive when she'd walked up. She'd expected him to take off when she'd left with the kids.

Maybe she should stop expecting things.

"Yeah. Had a life-altering epiphany, that's all."

"Anything I can help with?" he asked, shoving his hands into the pockets of his jeans.

She shook her head and stood. Sprocket stayed at her feet, waiting to see what she would do. "No. Thanks for sticking around. And for making them breakfast." She pulled off her hoodie, then walked close to Chris and the kitchen and saw he'd cleaned up. "And for doing the dishes."

"About that." He rubbed a hand over his head. "Listen, I didn't really think about it when I woke up and Kaden was staring at me. I didn't mean to overstep my boundaries. I figured you needed a few minutes of extra sleep. Kaden told me what time you walked them to the bus stop and I was going to wake you up as soon as I fixed their plates so you'd have time to get them there. I need you to know I wasn't—"

Grasping the sides of his face she pulled his head down to her, raising up on her tiptoes to close the distance—it was the easiest way to get him to shut up.

He stilled for a few seconds, possibly from shock, then wrapped one arm tightly around her waist while the other cradled her skull. Tilting her head, he took over the kiss, running his tongue along her bottom lip before sliding it into her mouth to tangle with hers.

Heat and tingles formed in her stomach and chest, expanding until they met with a whoosh, sending shock waves through her whole body. It wasn't only arousal—it was something more. Something she'd only felt with Chris. Something she couldn't define or put a name to yet. She still had some self-preservation instinct intact.

When he finally pulled away from their kiss, she was arched over his arm as if the force of his desire had slowly bent her to its will. Their chests rose and fell in unison, both of them breathless from the kiss.

Kiss. Such a silly word for what they'd done. There needed to be a better word for it. Something that described the over-whelming passion they'd shared. Since her brain wasn't firing on all synapses at the moment, she was having a hard time remembering her own name, much less coming up with a word to convey...that.

"Why'd you do that?" Chris asked.

His voice, a low, rough whisper, sent shivers across her skin and her already hard nipples puckered even more.

"You wouldn't stop talking."

"Denise—"

She pressed her lips to his again. It worked once. She didn't want to think about why she needed to kiss him, she just wanted to do it. To touch him and be touched.

He groaned against her mouth and moved the hand at her back lower, pressing her pelvis into his. The hard ridge of his erection rubbed against the junction of her thighs and she tilted her hips in an effort to get it closer to where she wanted it.

He groaned again and dragged his hand down the side of her neck to her chest, grasping and rubbing her breast through her shirt and sports bra. She moaned and arched back farther.

Chris moved his mouth to the tender spot at the corner of her jaw, nipping with his teeth. "Fuck, Denise. I want you so badly. I want to take you to the floor and bury myself in you. I want your legs wrapped around my hips while you squeeze my dick so fucking tight."

Her clit throbbed with the erotic picture he painted in her mind. "Holy shit."

"I won't fuck you on the floor again," he said.

Huh? "Why not?"

His hand returned to the back of her neck. "You started crying the last time."

Hello, cold bucket of water. Her eyes snapped open and found his. "You know that had nothing to do with you, right?"

"Yeah, but it was still pretty damn traumatic. Not sure if I'll ever be able to do it on the floor again."

She didn't know if he was completely serious or was trying to add some levity to a serious conversation. "How do you feel about couches?"

The corner of his mouth tilted up. "I like couches. I like beds even more."

Denise winced. "It's still Sarah's house and her bed. I'm not comfortable screwing around in her room."

His eyebrows rose. "But you're okay on the couch?"

"It's a couch. There's no telling how many butts those cushions have seen. And it's not as personal as her bed."

He nodded his head. "Couch it is." His grin was full of promise right before he kissed her again. He shuffled her toward the couch as a loud ping sounded from somewhere.

"Phone," he said.

"Not mine." She pushed up the hem of his t-shirt, the smooth expanse of his abs and chest hot and hard under her palms.

He yanked off his shirt and she leaned forward, flicking his hard nipple with the tip of her tongue. His hands fisted in her hair as he groaned.

The phone pinged again. "It's my phone," he said.

"Do you need to check it?" she asked, dragging her mouth across his chest to bite at his other nipple.

He hissed and she circled the flat disk with her tongue, eliciting a low growl.

"Shit."

"What?" She stood straight, knowing what he was going to say.

"I just looked at the clock. I have a meeting at nine so I need to leave in ten minutes. I have just enough time to get home to shower and change." He cradled her head, his thumbs brushing the along the hairline at her temple.

"Quickie?" A girl could hope.

He grinned and kissed her. Quickly. "I'd probably get off, but I'm pretty sure you wouldn't. I'm not going to be selfish like that." Another quick kiss.

She let out a low growl of frustration. While she appreciated his consideration, she was really fucking horny now. There was always the shower. It wouldn't be as satisfying but, oh well.

"Stay with me, Denise. I didn't say I wouldn't take care of you before I left." He reached around her and moved a couch pillow so it was close to the low armrest.

He positioned her near the end of the couch. "Lay back," he said with a small push on her shoulder.

Sitting on the arm of the sofa, she let out a gasp when he pushed her back. She stared up at Chris, her head lower than her hips and her legs hung over the side of the couch. Her clit throbbed as she realized what he intended to do.

Chris grasped the waist of her shorts and pulled them over her hips and thighs and down her legs, dragging her underwear with them. He licked his lips and flicked his gaze to hers. "You good?"

All she could do was nod. The anticipation was killing her. She might very well come as soon as he touched her. Her legs were restless and she wanted to rub them together to relieve some of the pressure but he was standing between them.

"Good." He bent at the waist and gripped her ass, tilting her hips to meet his hot, wet mouth.

Good. So good. He was a man on a mission. His tongue flicked and circled her clit. Pulling her closer to the edge of the armrest, he raised her legs and draped them over his shoulders, keeping her hips tilted.

One finger entered her and withdrew, then was joined by a second one. He twisted and thrust them while he continued to lick and suck on her clit.

She clutched the cushions next to her hips. So close. The pressure built in her belly, waiting for the right trigger to set her off.

He curled his fingers as he withdrew them. With his other hand, he circled her hood and sucked hard on her clit.

She exploded with a small cry. Throwing her head back, she squeezed his head with her thighs and rode his mouth and hands. Rolling her hips, her orgasm spiraled through her again and again. It became too much and she stopped squeezing and pushed at his head, trying to wiggle away.

He gripped her hips to keep her in place, but eased the pressure of his tongue, softly circling her clit before pulling away.

Peering at him through barely open eyes, she flushed when he wiped his mouth and chin, then wiped his hand on his jeans. She shouldn't be embarrassed by how wet she was—it was his fault.

She scooted back on the couch and he crawled over the arm, glancing at the decorative clock on the wall before laying on her and nestling between her legs.

"Six minutes," he said.

"That was it?" Should she be impressed with this skill or mortified by how quickly he could get her to come?

"What can I say?" He wagged his eyebrows. "I'm good."

She arched an eyebrow. There was no doubt, but she couldn't let his ego go unchecked. "Or it could be that I haven't had a session with B.O.B. in a couple of weeks."

His eyes darkened. "I'd like to watch that one day." Dropping his head, he nipped at her earlobe. "Watch how you get yourself off with your vibrator. How do you feel about using toys during sex?"

She thrust her hips against his. "You can't ask me things like that when you have less than four minutes until you have to leave."

His erection, bulging behind the seam of his jeans, dug into her sensitive flesh. "I know. I regretted it as soon as I asked, but it's true."

He raised his hips away from her and kissed her. It was softer. Gentle. He lingered with his lips pressed to hers before he ended it and laid his forehead against hers. "I don't know what we're doing, but I really want to keep doing it." He raised his head, his gaze searching hers. "Work, this case, it's crap. Noise that's doing its best to fuck this up. I want to ignore it and focus on what's going on right here between you and me."

Denise swallowed and took a deep breath. Time to leap or step back from the edge. That tight spot in her chest seemed to freeze, as if it didn't know if it was going to get tighter or finally begin to work itself loose. She licked her lips and swallowed again. "I want to figure out what we're doing."

Chris let out a breath and released all his weight, crushing her. "Thank fuck." He rose up on his elbows. "So…want to go on a date with me?"

Denise laughed and the knot began to loosen. "I have to take the kids on a date first. They haven't done anything fun for a few months and I promised them dinner and a movie."

"Okay. Let me know what day works for you." He glanced up. "And now I'm going to be late."

He pushed up from the couch and grabbed her shorts and underwear from the floor.

Sitting up, she took them from his outstretched hand and slid them back up her legs. She grabbed the pillow her hips had been on and tossed it toward the hall where the washer and dryer were.

Grabbing his keys from beside the door, he slid his feet into his shoes. Pulling her close, he kissed her. "Be safe. Call me if anything happens or you see anyone suspicious."

He had his work face on again. "I will."

His head reared back and he regarded her suspiciously. "Call me first if you end up shooting anyone, please."

She rolled her eyes.

Kissing her temple, he let her go to open the door.

"Chris?"

He turned back.

"Thank you for fixing the kids breakfast this morning."

"You're welcome." He winked and left.

CHAPTER 17

"*Y*ou can't bring that dog in here!" The young woman jumped up from her chair and moved behind it, using it as a barrier.

Denise glared at the girl and decided she hated her on sight. She was already annoyed at being called to the school in the middle of the day because Kimber had been sent to the principal's office. She'd had to ask Emily to stay and call in one of the volunteers because she didn't like leaving Emily by herself after Eddie's threat. Finding Kimber sitting in the outer office still crying had pissed her off even more. She was feeling stabby and this twenty-something, teacher-Barbie chick had put herself at the top of the list with her comment.

"Actually, according to titles two and three of the Americans with Disabilities Act, I can."

Sprocket, the dog in question, pawed at Denise's foot and leaned against her. She knew Denise was agitated and was trying to distract her. Unfortunately, this wasn't something she could be distracted from.

The man behind the desk stood and held out his hand. "Ms.

Reynolds, of course there's no issue with your service animal. I'm Mr. Silverman, the vice-principal. We didn't get a chance to meet when you came in to speak to Dr. Petersen."

Denise shook his hand, judging him by his soft and weak handshake. Blame it on too much time spent with people who knew the importance of establishing boundaries with the grip of a hand. She sat in the chair on the other side of his desk and Sprocket sprawled across her feet with her head pointed toward the door and Kimber.

"Why is my niece in the outer office crying?"

"Because she's a snotty brat," the young woman mumbled as she sat back down.

Denise white-knuckled the armrests of the chair to stay in it. "What did you say?" she asked through clenched teeth?

The girl crossed her arms. "Well, it's true. I don't care if her mom did just die."

"Are you fucking kidding me?" Denise looked at the vice-principal and pointed at the woman. "Who the fuck is she?"

"Ms. Reynolds, please watch your language."

"Answer the question." She wasn't going to dignify his request with a response. If she didn't start getting answers soon, she was going to drop f-bombs like she was carpet-bombing a Taliban stronghold in the Hindu Kush.

Mr. Silverman sighed. "This is Miss Neville, one of our elementary teachers."

"You let her teach children?"

"I'm a very good teacher," she said.

"Really?" Denise asked. "You think calling a student a brat makes you a good teacher? Call my niece names again, little girl, and I will end you. I will make it my personal mission to make your life a living hell. Are we clear?"

Sprocket whined and mouthed her ankle.

"Ms. Reynolds," the vice-principal said. "Please."

Denise looked back at him. "What. Happened?"

130

"Kimber was disrespectful to Ms. Neville during class," he said.

"In what way?" That didn't sound like Kimber at all.

"She argued with her in class."

"About what?"

"A math problem."

"A math problem?" She pursed her lips, tired of the politically correct game these people were trying to play. "Right. Get Kimber in here."

"Ms. Reynolds—"

"Get her in here. Now. I'm not playing this game. Since you refuse to give me a straight answer and explain the situation fully, I'll get it from her."

Looking extremely put out, he picked up his phone and asked the secretary to send in Kimber.

She had absolutely zero fucks to give. All her effort was going toward not unleashing unholy hell-fury on these assholes. She turned in the chair and watched Kimber hesitate in the doorway, looking between the adults in the room.

Denise held out her hand. "Come here, Kimber."

Kimber entered the office and stood beside her chair. Denise lifted her feet so Sprocket would move and pulled Kimber in front of her. "Tell me what happened in class today."

Kimber turned her head toward the teacher, her eyes downcast.

Swear to all that is holy, if that teacher threatened her, I'm taking a baseball bat to her car.

She grasped Kimber's chin and made her look at her. "Hey. Just you and me, okay? Tell *me*."

"We were doing math worksheets and I finished mine really fast, so Miss Neville started writing problems on the board and I kept getting them right. She kept putting harder and harder ones up and I was doing them. Then she put a really hard one on the board and she said, 'let's see you get this one, Smarty Pants.'"

The woman scoffed and Denise cut her eyes toward her,

daring her to open her mouth. She rolled her eyes and looked out the window.

Bitch.

"What happened then?" Denise asked.

"I got it right, but Miss Neville said I didn't. But I did! I know I did!"

"Okay, calm down." That was rich, coming from her. Oh well, those that can't do… "Where did the arguing come in?"

"I tried to show her what she did wrong, but she told me I didn't know what I was talking about because I'm just a kid. Then she sent me here and told Mr. Silverman I was d—d—disrespectful, but I wa—wasn't!"

Kimber threw herself into Denise's arms, crying almost hysterically. She'd always been sensitive and had never liked to be told she'd done something wrong. Being sent to the principal's office probably felt like being told she had to go to jail.

Denise patted her back and made shushing noises while glaring at the vice-principal. He rubbed his chin and looked at Miss Neville, as if this was the first time he'd heard Kimber's side of the story.

Dick.

She pulled Kimber away from her shoulder and whispered in her ear, "It's going to be okay. I'm very proud of you for sticking up for yourself."

Kimber hiccupped and stood upright. "Really?"

"Yes. Go wait outside."

She sniffed and wiped her cheek. "Can I take Sprocket?"

Denise took a deep breath. *She's a child. You're an adult. You can suck it up for five minutes.* "Yes."

Kimber bent and grasped Sprocket's short lead, taking her out with her.

Waiting until Kimber was in the outer office, she turned back to the teacher. "Was she right?"

The woman cut her eyes to the side. "That's not the point."

Denise shut her eyes, stretched her neck, and counted to five while blowing out a breath. "So let me get this straight—you got intimidated and embarrassed by an eight-year-old and your ego couldn't handle it. So instead of being a fucking adult about it, you abused your authority as her teacher to get her in trouble. That about it?"

She sulked and didn't respond.

You cannot throat punch her. "Is there another class Kimber can go into until we transfer at the end of the semester?" she asked the vice-principal.

"That won't be necessary. Miss Neville is a substitute and we won't be using her services after this incident."

"What?" Her outrage bordered on a shriek.

"Perhaps next time," Denise said as she stood, "you'll ask the student in trouble for their side of the story before deciding they should be punished. Just because someone is a child doesn't automatically mean they're lying any more than being an adult means someone is automatically telling the truth."

She left the office and went to the secretary's desk. "I'd like to pull Kaden out for the rest of the day. Can I go get him or does he need to be brought here?"

The older woman smiled. "I'll call down to his class and ask his teacher to send him here."

Sitting next to Kimber, she pulled out her phone and looked up the number her mom had sent her. Sprocket rose from her position on the floor and laid her head on her lap, looking up at her with her soulful eyes.

Denise closed her eyes while the phone rang and rubbed her dog's ears. The familiar gesture helped calm her emotions and lower her blood pressure. She timed the movement of her hand and pace of her breathing to the ringing in her ear.

On the fifth ring, it picked up. "Yumi Morris. May I help you?"

"Hi, Mrs. Morris. This is Denise Reynolds, Karen Reynolds's daughter?"

"Oh, yes! She said you might be calling. How are you?"

"I'm well, thank you." Kimber was watching her, so she smiled to let her know everything was all right. "I'm calling to see if you have time to fit me in this afternoon to come by to discuss enrolling Kimber and Kaden. I know it's very last minute, so I understand if today doesn't work."

"Hang on, let me see."

Denise leaned over and kissed Kimber on the head while she waited for Yumi to come back on the line.

"You're in luck, dear. I can move some things around if you can be here in the next thirty minutes."

Kaden entered the office and made a beeline for the chair next to Kimber, throwing his arm around her shoulders when he sat.

"We'll be there. Thank you so much."

"You're very welcome. I look forward to meeting you and your children."

Her heart squeezed a little tighter. Not in the way it usually did that left an ache. More like a pulse of happiness. *Her children.*

She stared at her cell phone for a moment, then looked at K-Squared. "Let's go on a field trip."

"SO, WHAT DID YOU THINK?" Denise asked as they walked out of the school toward the visitor parking lot.

Kimber skipped beside her. "It's awesome, Aunt Denny! They have a math club!"

"You're such a nerd," Kaden said.

"You're a geek," Kimber replied. "I saw you jump when Ms. Morris mentioned the robots."

"Robotics lab. Robots are cool."

"So's math."

"Is not."

"Is too."

"Guys!" Denise said. "Quit fighting. You are both smart and cool." Holy cow, how had Sarah handled this all the time? "I take it you both like the school."

"Yes!" they said in unison.

"When can we go here?" Kimber asked.

"Well, that's the thing," Denise said as they reached her SUV. "The plan was to wait until next year after we move to Bree's house during the summer. But if you guys want, we can see about moving sooner and you can transfer sooner."

She opened the back door and Sprocket jumped in, sitting in the center of the seat. The kids climbed in and Kimber got bathed in doggie kisses as she shuffled to the far side.

"You're letting us decide?" Kaden asked.

Denise leaned into the car. "Here's the deal. This affects you two, not me. You're the ones who have to move to a new house and change schools and leave all your friends behind. I want you to have a say in when we do it. I thought waiting until summer would be easier for you, but if you want to transfer now, I'll make it happen."

They looked at each other for a moment.

"I'll miss my friends," Kaden said. "But we'll make new ones."

"I'll only miss Melody and she can always come over to play on the weekends."

It was a lot to ask of them, to make a responsible decision like this, but she'd never had the option growing up. They'd just always moved. While they needed to move houses—and schools— she wanted them to feel like they were part of making the process happen instead of having the process happen to them.

"I really like this school," Kimber whispered.

"Me, too."

They looked at Denise. "Can we move tomorrow?" Kaden asked.

Denise laughed and ruffled his hair. "Not tomorrow, buddy. I need get you guys registered and make arrangements with Bree to move into her house. We can probably make it happen in a couple of weeks, though."

"Okay."

"Now that that's settled, how about if we go bowling?"

CHAPTER 18

"*P*leeeeease, Aunt Denny? It's my favorite song." Kimber folded her hands under her chin in supplication.

Denise's eye twitched. It was only a song. If she lived through the next three and a half minutes, she'd delete it from her music folder. *Oops. Sorry, honey, I don't know what happened.*

"One time. We're not listening to that song on repeat the whole way home."

"Yay!"

Kaden groaned. "Are you really going to make us listen to Taylor Swift?"

"Yes!" Kimber bounced up and down in her seat.

Denise pressed her thumb against the home button on her phone to unlock it and passed it back to Kimber. "Here you go." She turned south onto 401 as the first strains of *Shake It Off* came through the speakers, immediately regretting installing a new stereo system in her SUV.

"Aunt Denny," Kaden complained.

"Dude, I'll turn on Octane as soon as the song is done and let the soothing sounds of hard rock purge our eardrums. Deal?"

"Deal."

She glanced back at him through the rearview mirror. His arms were crossed and he was sulking, but his lips were moving, singing along to the song.

Pulling into a straightaway on the two-lane country road, she was nearly blinded by the high-beam headlights of a truck approaching from the rear. She was doing the speed limit, mindful that deer were prevalent on this stretch of road at night. The last thing she needed to do was take one out with the kids in the car.

She flipped the rearview mirror and put her hand up against the window to block the glare from the side mirror. "Go around, asshole," she muttered, slowing down so the driver could pass them.

Too late she realized he wasn't going to pass them.

"Shit!" She pressed the gas pedal, hoping to gain some speed before they were—

Crunch.

Kimber let out a little scream.

"What's happening, Aunt Denny?" Kaden asked.

She checked all the mirrors. The jolt had sent them forward, but the truck was approaching again. "I don't know, Kaden. Do me a favor. Turn off the music and dial nine-one-one."

"The screen's locked."

She hit the power button on the radio to shut off the music. In the sudden silence, she heard pipes approaching from the rear. Two Harley-Davidson motorcycles pulled alongside them as they were bumped again. Kimber screamed again and started crying.

"Guys, I need your help. I can't unlock the screen and drive. Kaden, hit the emergency call button and dial nine-one-one."

Sprocket growled low in her throat and snarled out the window.

"Sprocket, down. Go to Kimber."

One of the bikes pulled ahead of them and its taillight flashed, forcing her to brake so she didn't hit it.

"We're in my aunt's car. Someone is hitting us," Kaden said.

"Kaden, put it on speaker phone." She checked the rearview mirror. The truck was riding her bumper, only the dark silhouette of the driver visible.

"—what's your emergency?"

"My name is Denise Reynolds. I'm driving south on Highway 401, approaching Fayetteville. I have my niece and nephew in the car and we're being boxed in by two motorcycles and bumped by a truck behind us." A glance to the right showed no shoulder on the two-lane country highway. One of the reasons she loved this stretch of road was the lack of traffic. Fuck.

"Ma'am, your nephew said you were hit. Is that correct?"

She was losing speed trying not to hit the rider in front of her. Movement in her peripheral made her look left. The guy on the bike wore a mask that covered the lower half of his face and he was pointing a gun at her. He wagged it, telling her to pull over.

Her heart stuttered. She wasn't afraid of guns, she'd had more than a few pointed at her, but Kaden and Kimber hadn't. These motherfuckers were putting her kids in danger. Just bumping her to make her lose control had been enough of a risk.

"Guys, keep your seat belts on and lay on the seat." Her fingers itched to pull her own gun and point back, but Kimber's muffled sobs stopped her. Shooting the asshole wasn't an option with the kids in the car. Sprocket's tags jangled, but she couldn't take the chance to look.

"Ma'am, please don't make any aggressive moves toward the other vehicles. Proceed as quickly and safely as possible to the nearest police station."

Fuck that noise. "Right. 'Cause I know exactly where that is. Kaden, the pass code to my phone is one-two-three-five-eight-zero. Can you find the map app and find a police station?"

She eased down on the gas pedal, slowly picking up speed,

forcing the bike in front of her to do the same or get bumped himself. His taillight flashed, but she ignored it. His bike jolted forward and wobbled when she refused to back down. A quick glance out of the corner of her eye showed her the guy on her left had become more insistent with his signal to pull over.

"I think so."

Another bump from behind snapped her neck forward. These assholes were seriously beginning to piss her off. A "curve ahead" road sign flashed by and she knew exactly where they were. A large culvert ran perpendicular to this particular section of highway. All she needed to do was clear the path ahead of them and pick up some speed.

And hope the asshole on the bike didn't try to shoot out her tires.

"Okay. Hang on. I'm getting us out of here."

The voice on the phone continued to babble, but she wasn't listening.

She didn't ease down on the pedal—she floored it. The maneuver knocked the bike in front of them, sending it sideways and crashing to the pavement. Braking hard, she swerved to the left, sending the gunman into the guardrail along the road. Then she hit the gas again. The screech of brakes echoed as she picked up speed. Checking the rearview quickly, she saw the truck stopped in the road behind them. Guess they were lucky the driver hadn't been willing to run over his buddies.

She turned the headlights off, taking her chances with the ambient light cast by random street and house lights.

"In four hundred feet, turn left," the map's automated voice said.

Noting the odometer, she waited until the last minute before slowing down to make the turn.

"You guys okay?"

"Yes," they both said.

"Ma'am, are you still there?"

She reached between the seats and held out her hand. "Let me have the phone, buddy."

He placed it in her hand. "Where'd you learn to drive like that?"

"The Army."

"Cool."

Well, shit.

Denise sat at the utilitarian table, absentmindedly scratching Sprocket's head. Damn good thing they'd let her keep her dog with her. She'd be losing her shit about now if not. It was bad enough they'd separated her from the kids. The only reason she'd allowed that to happen was her parents had shown up at the police station right before the FBI agents.

The door opened and the agents from earlier walked in. They both wore black suits and she fought to roll her eyes at the *Men in Black* cliché they presented. Something about one or both of them set Sprocket off, making her hackles rise and she growled low in her throat.

"Control your dog," the woman agent said.

Huh. She wouldn't have pegged her as the problem child. Not a good way to start an interrogation of a witness. *Amateur.* "She doesn't like you," she said pleasantly.

"We'll remove it if we have to," she threatened.

"You're welcome to try."

Chris and Phil walked in and sat across from her at the table. Phil nodded tightly and she responded with a small smile. From Chris she got nothing. Not even a good evening. And wasn't that just the icing on tonight's cake.

"Ms. Reynolds—Denise. Please bring your dog to heel," Phil asked.

"Sprocket."

The dog immediately sat and licked her chops but the hair on her nape was still raised with her agitation.

"It's nice to see you again, even if it's under these circumstances. We appreciate your cooperation."

Denise glanced between Chris and Phil and then at the agents who'd taken up positions around the room, effectively boxing her in, and raised an eyebrow. "Do you?"

"We do," Chris said. His voice was flat. Even. No stress to indicate he was anything more than an agent questioning a witness.

Denise pressed her lips together and cut her eyes to the side. "I'd appreciate it if there was no one standing behind me." The third agent was beside the door so she could see him in her periphery, but the female agent had taken up residence behind her and she could feel her animosity looming over her.

Phil glanced over Denise's shoulder and nodded his head to the side. She swore she felt her hair shift in the breeze created by the agent's sigh, but she moved.

"What do you need?" Denise asked. She'd cooperate as long as it was in her and K-Squared's best interests.

"Run through what happened," Chris said.

Another look gave her no indication of what he was feeling. Just another day at the office. The ache that throbbed in her chest made her realize it had gone away—for a while at least. Now it was back. She really needed to learn her lesson the first few times.

Mentally shaking her head, Denise spread her hands flat on the table, fingers splayed, and closed her eyes. She needed to give them the details and take Kaden and Kimber home where they were safe.

She went through S.A.L.U.T.E. – Size, Activity, Location, Unit, Time, and Equipment. Old habits died hard and reporting enemy actions had once been second nature. She froze the moment in her mind, examining it from every angle and running back over the details she'd filed away to recall later. She went through the timeline from the first time they were hit until they pulled into the police station.

"The bike on my side had custom artwork on the gas tank. Yellow or gold flames. I couldn't see any artwork on the one in front of me. They had on black helmets and the faces were covered by those half masks that look like skulls. Long sleeve black shirts and jeans on one of the guys, black pants on the other. They were both wearing leather vests with Southern Anarchist patches on the back."

Sprocket whined and jumped up on her lap, licking her chin.

She opened her eyes and scratched her behind the ears. She glanced at Chris. His bright blue eyes were intense. They flicked to his right, toward the female agent and he dropped his gaze to the notepad in his hands.

Right. The job. That's why he was here. How could she forget?

"Why didn't you pull your gun?" the agent by the door asked.

She'd told the cops who'd been waiting for them that she'd had a handgun stashed on the side of her seat. "I didn't feel it was prudent to draw my weapon with the kids in the car."

"You have five handguns registered in your name," he said.

"Yes."

"You don't think that's a bit many for a woman?"

Oh hell no. "How many do you have?" she asked.

"I have two." He crossed his arms defensively and leaned against the door jamb.

"Don't you think that's too few for a man?" she snarked.

Phil snorted and then coughed into his hand. "Sorry. Allergies."

Denise found her first genuine smile that night. "What can I say? I'm an ammo-sexual who likes to exercise my Second Amendment rights."

The agent rolled his eyes and grimaced.

"Eddie Perry," Chris said.

It was the first time he'd looked directly at her for more than a few seconds and she wished he'd just kept looking at his notepad.

Two days ago, he'd had his face buried between her legs, making her promises, and now he treated her like a stranger. Objectively she understood what he was doing, not showing any emotion or hinting at any personal connection, especially in front of other agents, but she was so tired of it. Tired of being second. Tired of always being promised more, when there wasn't any.

"What about him?"

"You think he was involved in this?"

"After demanding to know where his kids are and the threats he made at the rescue, yes—he was involved in this. I don't know if he was one of the guys on the bikes or if he was in the truck or if he was even there at all, but he was involved somehow. There is no reason for them to target me otherwise."

"I'm sure you're aware of the FBI's interest in the Southern Anarchists," Phil said.

"I am aware."

"We believe Eddie Perry is making a play to take over the Anarchists," Chris said. "We've had several reports he's trying to reconstitute the group under his leadership with intentions to branch out into guns, drugs, and human trafficking."

She didn't respond. Partly because she couldn't make herself care. What the Anarchists did wasn't her problem. Keeping Eddie away from Kimber and Kaden was her problem and she wasn't going to do anything to put them in the middle of a war between the FBI and the Anarchists. She waited, content to sit in the silence, knowing eventually someone would say something to fill the void. People tended to be uncomfortable with silence, especially after a statement had been made to elicit a response.

They knew that. They'd had similar training to what she'd had, but with the exception of Chris they likely didn't know her background. She'd sat for hours across from a detainee fighting a silent battle of wills. She'd never lost.

"Jesus! Don't you care?" the female agent asked.

"No. I don't," she said. "Eddie Perry can rot in hell. I wish you all the luck in catching him and the rest of the Anarchists but, other than their threat to my kids, I don't have shit to do with them."

"We'd like to put you and the children in a safe house," Phil said.

"No."

"Denise—"

Denise leaned forward in the chair and braced her arms on the table. "I said no. These kids have had their lives disrupted enough in the past few weeks. They know nothing about their biological father and now I have to tell them the boogeyman exists. You want to put a detail on them, that's fine. I'll even give you access to the house if your true concern is their safety. But I'm going to keep their lives as normal as I possibly can."

That wasn't entirely true. She'd take the kids and go off-grid if she needed to. She held Phil's gaze, unwilling to give an inch.

He sighed and nodded. "As you wish. We'll assign a detail to watch your house and their school."

Denise nodded and leaned back in her seat. She needed to tell Graham so his guys would be aware there'd be a second team. "Is there anything else you need from me tonight? I need to get the kids home and in bed—they have school in the morning and it's been a very long day for them."

"Your parents took them home about half an hour ago," Phil said.

Her chest tightened. She knew they were safe with her dad, but the idea of them being out there without her still sent a fissure of worry through her. Sprocket nuzzled her hand, lifting her palm with her snout.

Standing, she gave Sprocket the command to *block*. The dog followed her from the interrogation room, keeping her rear protected. Not that she expected the agents to jump her, but she was still on edge from the attack earlier—hyperaware and hypersensitive to all the people moving around her. The tiny pinpricks of hurt feelings weren't helping matters.

Taking her phone from the small locker they'd asked her to leave it in, she turned it on and waited for it to boot up. Pulling up a hidden app, she checked to see if they'd messed with her phone. Not that she didn't trust the FBI but...she didn't trust the FBI. Either they hadn't tampered with her phone or they used a program the app couldn't detect. She'd hook it up to her laptop later and run a scan.

Denise sensed Chris the moment he left the interrogation room. Their gazes locked. Finally, he showed some emotion, anger blazing from his eyes. From her refusal to help or her refusal to put the kids in a safe house, she didn't know. She couldn't work up the energy to care.

Phil exited the room and stopped in front of her, handing her his card. "Just in case you need it. The safe house offer is good anytime you change your mind."

"Thanks." She shoved the card in her back pocket and pivoted toward the exit. She had people to take care of at home.

CHAPTER 19

*D*enise pulled into the Walgreens parking lot and drove around to the back of the building. Leaving the engine running, she set the brake and took a small flashlight from the center console. She got out and scanned the area. Clicking on the flashlight, she dropped onto her hands and knees and shined the light under the front bumper. She repeated the process for the rear bumper and the wheel wells. Tucked into the rear passenger wheel well, she found what she was looking for.

She pushed up from the ground and got back in her SUV, locking the doors. Sprocket hung her head between the seats as Denise examined the small device she'd found. The GPS tracker was about the size of a large key fob with three LED lights on the front. The middle yellow light was lit, possibly indicating that the battery was dying. She flipped it over, trying to find a power switch. Not finding one, she pulled out her knife from the console and flipped it open. She ran the edge along the seam of the small box, separating the two halves. Slipping the knife under the wires, she flicked the tip and detached the ends of the leads. She checked to make sure no light was showing and threw the pieces onto the passenger seat.

TARINA DEATON

Assholes had tagged her car.

Denise released the brake and shifted into gear, heading to back to the house. She had to talk to her parents—they needed to decide on a course of action for protecting the kids. An FBI safe house might be the logical solution, but it didn't feel like the right one and it would cut her off from her support network. She might be able to trust Chris, but she didn't know his coworkers and, more than that, she needed her parents and Bree around her.

Pulling in beside her dad's extended-cab pickup, she shut off the engine and gathered up the pieces of the GPS. She let Sprocket out of the back and thumbed the lock on her doors out of habit. It wouldn't stop anyone from breaking in, but that was no reason to make it easy on them.

She unlocked the door and pushed it open with her shoulder. Sprocket glanced up at her and then made a beeline for the couch and Kimber and Kaden. They'd had a bath and were in their pajamas watching cartoons.

No sooner had she thrown the dead bolt than Sprocket let out a short woof and looked at the door. A brief knock followed. She checked the peephole and opened the door for Chris.

"What—"

He grasped her face and kissed her. His mouth held an edge of desperation, as if he was trying to pour all his anger and worry into the kiss. She stiffened and pushed against his chest.

"What are you doing?"

"I'm sorry." He rested his forehead against hers. "It took everything I had not to do this when we walked into that room, but I can't chance being taken off this case. There's too much riding on it."

Her emotions clashed inside her like Titans battling for Olympus. Hope and defeat. Her heart screamed that he was apologizing, but her mind had kicked her feet up on the desk and was filing her fingernails, wondering *so the fuck what*.

She wanted this and if she were honest with herself, she'd

148

wanted it as soon as he'd walked into that interrogation room. Care. Comfort. Support. Someone to stand beside her and guard her back if she needed it. Someone who knew she could handle herself, but still worried enough that the first thing he did when he saw her was devour her in an effort to prove to himself she was safe. But what did she have to do before someone just supported her when she needed it instead of assuming she had things covered?

Giggling reminded her they had an audience. "Now's not the time to talk about this."

"Denise—"

A throat cleared behind her. Chris raised his head and searched her gaze before turning to look at her father.

"Son, I'm going to have to ask what your intentions are toward my daughter." Her father stood with his hands on his hips, feet braced apart. She knew that stance. It was the one he'd taken when she was growing up and had to explain herself when she'd done something he thought she shouldn't have.

She forced a smile. "Why don't you ask me what my intentions are toward him?" She tried to move back a step, but Chris kept his arm wrapped around her.

Her father shifted his piercing gaze to her, not missing anything, and playing along anyway. "Good point. Denise, what are your intentions toward this young man?"

Denise rolled her eyes. "Pretty sure I'm never sharing any of my intentions with you."

Kimber, now peeking over the back of the couch watching the show by the door, giggled again. "I told you he was her boyfriend." Kaden scrunched his face up as if to say "ew, gross" and turned back around to watch the TV.

"We did agree to go steady," Chris said.

"I agreed to go on a date," she replied.

He shrugged. "Same thing." He released her, but kept one arm around her waist. "Sir, I intend on dating your daughter."

"Ha! Good luck with that." Her father dropped his hands and went back into the kitchen, passing her mother on the way.

Denise rubbed her eyebrow. How the hell had she gotten into this mess? More importantly, how could she get out of it without causing a scene?

"Leave her alone, Frank." Her mom smacked her dad on the stomach. "It's good to see you again, Chris."

"You too, Mrs. Reynolds." He released his hold on Denise's waist.

"Karen, please." She wrapped her arms around Denise and hugged her tight.

Denise closed her eyes and breathed in the muted scent of her mother's perfume. She needed this. It brought back memories of sitting on her lap as a little girl, wishing her nails were long and elegant like her mom's, and that she liked the things her mom liked. She'd never been that girly-girl and she'd always worried she disappointed her mom, right up until she was thirteen years old and she overheard her mom bragging to one of her friends about how she was the only girl to make the Little League team.

Jeez, where had that come from? She needed some couch time with Dr. Tailor. Her whole sense of balance was out of whack.

Her mom rubbed her back and let her go. "I saved you some dinner. It's just spaghetti, but I wanted to make something quick the kids would eat."

"Did they eat already?" Denise asked.

"Yes. I told them they could stay up a little longer and wait for you to come home."

"How are they doing?" She dropped her voice to barely a whisper.

Her mom glanced at them. "They seem to be doing okay. They were worried about when you were going to be home," she said in the same whisper.

Denise nodded and glanced at the clock above the television. They were already thirty minutes past their bedtime. She needed to make sure they kept their normal schedule. Normal was important for all of them. "Alright, monkeys, pause your show if you want to save it. It's time for bed."

"Can Grandma read stories with us tonight?" Kimber asked.

"I want Aunt Denny to read to us," Kaden said.

She could see the fight brewing. "How about if you read to Grandma while I eat dinner and then I'll read to you?"

They looked at each other as if having a silent conversation. "Okay," Kaden said.

"All right. Teeth. Bathroom. Bed. Ready? Break." Denise clapped her hands and the kids scrambled off the bed, racing each other to the bathroom.

"We're reading The *Magic Tree House* series," she told her mom. "It's on the table between their beds."

"Sarah loved that series." Her mom's eyes grew teary.

Denise kissed her on the cheek. "I'm pretty sure they're the same books."

Her mom wiped a tear away and took a deep breath. Pivoting toward the bedrooms, she called out, "All right, kids, let's check those teeth."

She smiled after her mom for a moment, before pulling herself back to reality. "Let's go in the kitchen."

Chris stayed close behind her with his hand low on her back. Her dad leaned against the counter in front of the sink with his arms crossed. She went to him and he wrapped her in his arms. It was different than her the way her mom had, but it was just as comforting.

"I liked it better when I didn't know the shit you were getting into," he said, gruffly.

She huffed out a small laugh and raised her head from his chest. They'd never talked about what she'd done in Iraq or Afghanistan. He simply told her he was there if she needed to talk to someone who'd been there, too. She loved her dad, had been a daddy's girl growing up, but there were some things she hadn't been able to share with him.

"How'd they find you?" he asked when she pulled back.

"I wondered the same thing," she said. "There was no way they should have known where we were going to be and I never spotted anyone following us. The trip to the new school was a spur of the moment decision and it's not like I'm on a bowling league." She pulled the disabled GPS from her jeans pocket and held it out in her palm. "Found this in one of the wheel wells."

Her dad took it from her and turned it over in his hands, examining it then passed it to Chris.

She didn't know what to make of her dad including Chris in the discussion. Because he was FBI or for other reasons?

"How long do you think it's been there?" her dad asked.

"No idea. It didn't even occur to me to sweep my car."

"It looks off-the-shelf. Battery probably wouldn't last more than ten days—maybe a couple more if it wasn't on all the time," Chris said.

"There was a yellow light lit when I found it."

"Probably indicates the amount of charge." He tossed the device on the counter. "I think you should reconsider the safe house."

"I can't cut myself off from parents or Bree, which I'd have to do going into a safe house."

"Cabin?" her dad asked.

She shook her head. "Not unless we absolutely have to. Kaden and Kimber have been through enough already. I don't want to disrupt their lives any more than necessary."

"You want me and your mom here at night?"

Denise smiled at the image of her dad trying to get comfortable on Sarah's Goodwill couch. "There's no room for you here. The FBI is going to put surveillance on us, anyway."

"Denise, they probably know where you live. One team isn't going to do much if they decide to raid this house."

True, but she also had Graham's team. Since she wasn't ready to share that information yet, she tried to reassure him. "I know. I'll talk to Bree and see if we can move to her house sooner than we planned. The alarm system she had installed is state of the art. In that neighborhood, someone will call the cops if they see something out of the norm. Unlike here, where Eddie and his friends blend right in."

"You need to tell them about Eddie," her dad said.

"I know, but not tonight. Tomorrow after school, when we have time to explain and answer all their questions. I need you and Mom there with me."

"Whatever you need," her dad promised.

"Thanks, Dad."

"I'm proud of you, baby girl."

The backs of her eyes stung and she blinked to stop the tears from forming. She hadn't been the easiest person to deal with when she'd gotten out of the Army and had put her parents through some serious shit. Cutting herself off from them had been easier than admitting she needed help. She'd come a long way since then and it meant a lot for her dad to say that.

Afraid if she tried to say anything she'd choke on the tears sitting in the back of her throat, she nodded.

"I'm gonna go say goodnight to the kiddos." He kissed her on the forehead and patted her hip. "Let your mom know when you want us here."

"Will do."

Chris tried to pull her into his arms and but she side-stepped to get a glass from the cupboard.

"What are you thinking?" he asked.

She filled the glass with water and took a long drink. She could talk to him about her plan. For whatever reason he was there—the job or her—she needed to air her concerns. It wasn't weakness to admit doubts or question the chosen course of action. A good leader listened to advice and took counsel from others.

"Wondering if I'm making the right decision by not tucking them away somewhere. Going over the defenses of the house."

He leaned a hip against the counter and crossed his arms. "I'm not going to lie—I want to put y'all in my truck and drive you as far away from here as I can."

"It's not your decision."

His eyes darkened and he looked down, then back up. "This house isn't very safe."

"No. Their room especially. Single story, low window with flimsy locks."

"You sleeping on the floor in there tonight?"

"I'm going to move them into my room after my parents leave."

He nodded. "I'll sleep on the couch again. Phil's in a car one block over. There's another team set up at the top of the subdivision."

"Seems like an awful lot for one guy," she said.

Chris rubbed his hands over his face. "The Southern Anarchists ran guns and drugs for years. About two years ago, they branched out into human trafficking. Kids, Denise. Girls as young as twelve. Some of the shit I saw when I was undercover... And they assassinated two of our people."

Jesus, she felt like a cold-hearted bitch. It was easy to think she couldn't do anything about those kids, but that wasn't true.

She could.

She could make it easy for Eddie to get close so the FBI could grab him. But that meant putting Kaden and Kimber in harm's way and she wouldn't do it. As horrible as it made her, she wouldn't put her kids at risk for a faceless, nameless stranger.

"Why do you think Eddie is the key to this?"

He shook his head. "Honestly? I don't know that I do, but right now he's the only lead we have. The group broke up and spread out after the bust. Our intel tells us he's gathering all the squirters back together. Whether he's going to continue where they left off or take them back to what they were doing when he was VP or in a different direction, we don't know. But we can't risk them getting another foothold in this area and reestablishing their distribution lines. There's too much at stake."

This was important to him and she knew why, but there were chances she wasn't willing to take again. "Are you mad I won't go along with what the FBI wants?"

He moved closer and put his hands on the counter by her hips. "No. I know why you're doing what you're doing and I don't fault you for it. Do I want to bundle you up and put you all in the safe house so you're protected? Abso-fucking-lutely. But this is my job —not yours."

She held his gaze, wanting to believe what he said was true. To believe in *him*, but he'd said it himself. It was his job.

So much of what was happening now echoed what had happened in Iraq it was hard not to draw parallels. To not think the universe was doling out one major mind fuck. Maybe it was giving her a second chance to do it right this time. What if she made the wrong decision, though? What if she was making the wrong decision now?

No, she was in a better position in familiar territory than someplace she didn't know with strangers whose motives she didn't understand. She'd chosen a plan and she'd stick to it until she had to adjust course.

"I'll take the kids to school and pick them up. No more riding the bus. They're with me, my parents, or Bree. I know Bree will let us move in this week, even if it's just clothes for the moment."

He held her gaze for a moment. "When were you planning on moving?"

"At the end of the school year to make it easier for the kids to adjust, but they really liked the school we toured and they can start next week."

"They okay with that?"

Denise smiled a half smile. "After what happened, yes."

"Denise, honey," her mom called from the living room, snapping her out of her thoughts. "They're ready for you to read to them."

"Be right there," she said over her shoulder. She pushed against his arms to move away from the counter. "I'm going to walk them out, then read to the kids."

He followed her into the living room and shook hands with her dad. He got a double clap on the shoulder, which surprised her. That was her dad's signature *I like this guy* gesture usually reserved for old Army buddies.

She hugged her parents and told her dad to stop somewhere along the way and check for a tracking device.

"Who taught you what you know?" he asked.

All she could do was roll her eyes.

"We'll be back tomorrow afternoon," her mom said. "We can stay with the kids if you need to go back to work."

Damn. She'd forgotten about work. Something else she needed to talk to Bree about. The rescue needed help. An office manager wouldn't be a bad idea. They'd gotten big enough that she was having a hard time keeping up with the paperwork and the training.

She waited in the doorway until her parents turned the corner. The deadbolt seemed to echo when she turned it, locking Chris in the house with her. Even with all her doubts, it felt right having him there with her at the end of the night. If only she knew for sure he wasn't there out of obligation to his job.

CHAPTER 20

*D*enise heard the rustle of sheets and tensed. Cracking open an eyelid, she peered at Kimber crawling off the bed and kneeling down next to her on the floor.

Relief made her muscles loose. Extra bodies was yet another thing she was going to have to get used to. She shifted onto her back and stretched her arm out, inviting Kimber to snuggle close. The little girl rested her head in the pocket of Denise's shoulder and threw her arm across her stomach.

"Do we have to go to school today?" she whispered.

Denise kissed the top of her head and sniffed the subtle watermelon scent of the kids shampoo they used. She'd had the same thought last night after moving them to her bed. She was still undecided.

"Why don't you want to go to school?'

"It's boring," Kimber said. "I finish all my work really fast and then there's nothing to do until the next lesson."

Truthfully, she'd rather have them with her all day even if it meant taking them to the rescue. "How about this? I'll call the principal and ask for your and Kaden's assignments for the rest of the week and you guys can hang out at the rescue with me during the day. After you finish your schoolwork, you can help me with the dogs."

"Really?" Kaden hung his head over the side of the bed, staring down at them with a huge grin.

She smiled back and shook her head at him. "Really. It's only two more days and next week you should be at your new school." *Note to self: call Bree this morning.* She needed to make sure Bree was good with them moving this weekend. At the very least, she could use the address and drive the kids to school if she had to.

"Yay!" Kaden scrambled up and jumped up and down on the bed.

Kimber squeezed her tight and let out a small squeak.

Denise smiled at how easy it was to make them happy. Her joy was marred by the twinge in her back that reminded her she was sleeping on the floor and why. She rubbed her eyes. She should talk to them this morning before they went to the rescue.

Patting Kimber's shoulder, she rolled up. "All right. Quit jumping before you break the bed. Go put clothes on while I start breakfast."

Kaden jumped one more time, landing on his butt, and launching himself off the bed. She winced when he missed the corner of the wall by inches. *Note to self: research health insurance for the kids.* She was running out of mental sticky notes. *Note to self: write all this shit down.*

"Aunt Denny! Mr. Chris is asleep on the couch again," Kaden yelled.

"Not anymore he's not," Denise mumbled. "I know, honey. He stayed to make sure we were safe after what happened yesterday."

Standing up, she braced a hand on the back of her hip and twisted, cracking her lower back. Shooing Kimber in front of her and out of the bedroom, she pulled her hair up into a messy bun and secured it with the hair tie from around her wrist.

"Why did he have to make sure we're safe?" Kimber asked.

Denise stared down her. Should she tell them now or wait

until later? She looked up and found Chris watching her from the couch.

God, he was sexy in the morning. His early scruff had a slight tinge of red and framed his lips perfectly. It'd taken all her energy last night not to kiss him goodnight. It wouldn't have been a simple kiss and after yesterday morning, she didn't think she had the willpower to stop it from going further. She couldn't afford to be that distracted with the kids so close in the next room.

"Why don't I make breakfast?" He stood and shuffled into the kitchen.

Distracted like that. "Okay, new plan. We're going to talk first and then we'll get dressed and have breakfast."

She herded them onto the couch, pulled the coffee table close, and sat facing them. Her parents were supposed to be here to help her get through this. She couldn't keep relying on other people as the first line of defense. They needed to be backup, not the primary response. How was she supposed to start this conversation?

"Is this a grown-up talk?" Kaden asked.

"What's a grown-up talk?"

"You know, when you tell us serious stuff like we're grown-ups," Kimber said.

"Did your mom have grown-up talks with you?"

"Yeah. But only when it was something really important," Kaden said.

"Like what?" She was woefully unprepared for the responsibility Sarah had left her.

It was her own fault. She'd assumed her parents would get guardianship and they'd already done it twice. They were pros. She'd just had to figure things out until they took over. Sarah had been too weak to give her all the sage parenting advice she needed by the time she dropped that bombshell on Denise. All her will had stated was Denise got custody and her dad was the executor of her estate.

Note to self: Google "how not to fuck up parenting." That should cover everything.

"Private parts are private and only pacific people should see them," Kimber said.

"Specific people."

"Right, pacific people."

Denise pressed her lips together. Did laughing at your kids fall under being a shit parent? "What else?"

"Don't talk to shifty people," Kaden said.

She frowned. Was that another misspeak? "Who are shifty people?"

"Grown-ups who ask kids for help," Kaden said.

"And kids who ask you to go with them to help them. They should ask a grown-up for help." Kimber said.

"And not to trust grown-ups who say Mom sent them to pick us up," Kimber said.

"They're supposed to know our code word," Kaden said.

Denise blinked at them. "How come I don't know your code word?"

"'Cause you're family, silly," Kimber said. "Family doesn't need to know the code word."

"Ah. That makes sense."

"Mom told me our dad was a shifty person," Kaden said. "She said he died, too, but that man who called said he was our dad. Was that a lie?"

There was the segue she needed. Taking a deep breath, she tried to explain. "Sometimes, grown-ups tell people lies because the truth is really bad or it might really hurt the other person's feelings."

"Mommy lied to us?" Kimber asked.

She moved closer so her knees were touching theirs and took their hands. "To answer your first question, yes, this is going to be a grown-up talk. Your mommy lied to you a little bit, but it was to protect you from a really bad truth."

Trying to frame the words as gently as possible, she gave their hands a squeeze. "Your dad —" God, she hated using that word "— was a bad man. He did some illegal things and hurt some people, including your mom. One day he hurt her really bad and another man tried to help, but your dad hurt him, too. The police sent your dad to prison for a very long time. We think the men yesterday were some of your dad's friends."

She glanced toward the kitchen. Chris leaned against the low counter, arms crossed. His emotions played across his face from anger to worry to *I'm here if you need me.* He gave her an unexpected sense of comfort.

"But those men tried to hurt us," Kimber said.

Denise could see the confusion and hurt on her face. "I think they meant to scare us, sweetie, not hurt us."

Them, maybe. Anything that happened to her was probably considered collateral damage.

"Why would he do that?" Kaden asked. "Why would he hurt mommy and why would he let his friends scare us?"

She rubbed the back of his small hand. "I don't know, sweetheart."

"Is he going to hurt us?" Kimber asked.

"I will not let that happen," she said. "I promise." She prayed it was a promise she'd be able to keep.

THE KIDS WERE SUBDUED while they did their schoolwork. The principal had been more than willing to send the week's remaining assignments to her along with the paperwork to disenroll them and transfer their records to their new school. She tried working up some annoyance at the principal so willing to not deal with an issue, but it made her life easier so in the end she decided to let it go. The kids were happy and excited about their new school so she'd take the good where she could get it.

She sent a quick text to Bree. *Got time to talk?*

Bree: About 5 mins between patients. What's up?

Will need more time than that.

Bree: Everything ok?

Wasn't that the sixty-four-thousand-dollar question?

Need more than 5 mins. Call me at lunch?

Bree: Will do

She saved the financial spreadsheet she'd been working on and locked the computer screen. Tucking her phone into her pocket, she left her small office to check on the kids working at the small break table.

"How's it going?"

"How much longer do we have to do this?" Kaden asked with a groan.

She chuckled at his ire. They'd been at it for less than two hours. "That depends. How much do you have done?"

"All the reading and most of the math," he said.

"I have all the math and social studies done," Kimber said. "I finished the reading last week."

"Nerd."

"Geek." Kimber stuck her tongue out at Kaden.

"No fighting," she said automatically. She scanned the syllabus for their classes and compared it to what they had done. "How about a break? Do you guys want to take some of the rescues out into the field while I clean out their kennels?"

"Yes!" They both jumped up and down in their seats.

"First, I want to introduce you to one of the dogs."

They followed her to Sweetpea's pen. The tan and white dog immediately stood and did her butt wiggle when she realized they were coming to her.

Denise unlatched the chain link door and knelt down. "I've been calling her Sweetpea because she's so sweet."

She pulled her chin back out of licking distance as the dog

tried to crawl in her lap. Kimber and Kaden crouched next to her and petted the dog.

"Whose dog is she?" Kimber asked.

"Well, I was thinking when we move we could take her with us and she could be your dog," she said.

Both kids froze and stared at her wide-eyed. "Really?" Kaden asked.

"Really."

They lunged at her and threw their arms around her neck. Off balance from their combined weight and momentum, she fell backward and was quickly overtaken by kids and dog.

She pulled her knees up to protect her stomach from Sweetpea's pointy paws. "I take it that's a yes."

"Yes! Yes! Yes!"

Kimber peppered her cheek with kisses while Kaden untangled himself from Denise and hugged Sweetpea instead. At least she knew her place in his priorities.

She leveraged up and stood once Kimber had turned her attention to Sweetpea.

"Can we take her out now?" Kaden asked.

"Yes. She's good with the group we're starting with. Grab her lead from the hook while I get the other dogs."

She let Emily know she was taking the kids across to the barn. Kaden and Kimber followed her out the side door and across the yard, Sprocket lumbering along beside them. They played with the foster dogs in groups until the alarm on her phone beeped, reminding her it was almost lunchtime.

"Let's get your books from the office and we'll go up to my apartment for lunch."

"Can we bring Sweetpea up with us or does she have to go back into her kennel, too?" Kaden asked.

She closed the final dog's stall door. "She can come."

"Yay."

Sprocket rolled up from her spot in the shade and followed them to the office, then upstairs to Denise's apartment.

She hadn't been there in almost a week and the air was stale and musty. No telling what the inside of her fridge would look like.

"Have you guys done your science homework yet? 'Cause I think I have some experiments you can use in here."

Kimber giggled from her seat at the table.

Denise closed the refrigerator door and opened the freezer. "Mac and cheese or pizza?"

"Pizza," they both said.

Thank goodness they were easy. She pulled the frozen pizza out and set the oven to preheat. "Work on your schoolwork while the oven heats."

"Awww. Can't we watch TV for a while?" Kaden asked.

She cocked a hip against the counter and folded her arms. "I'll make a deal with you. You work until two o'clock and I'll let you watch TV."

He squinted his eyes at her and mirrored her crossed arms. "Does that include taking a break to eat pizza?"

"That includes eating pizza between answering social studies questions."

He dropped his arms and sagged his shoulders. "Ugh."

Kimber had already pulled her books out of her book bag and set them on the small table.

"Think of it as practice for college," Denise said.

"I'm not going to college. I'm going to join the Army like you and Grandpa."

A montage of her years in the Army flashed through her mind. She was in no way prepared to overlay her nine-year-old nephew into any of those scenes. "We'll talk about that when you're eighteen. And either way, you're still going to have to learn to study while eating pizza. It's a life skill. Right up there with learning how to drive a stick shift."

"What's a stick shift?" he asked.

"Oh, young Padawan, you have much to learn."

"What's a Padawan?"

She dropped her arms in shock. "What's a—Well, I know what you're going to be watching on TV for the next week." Her phone vibrated in her back pocket before she could delve further into the severe lack of their cultural education.

Bree's grinning face stared at her from the screen and she slid her thumb across it. "Hey. Hang on a sec." She lowered the phone. "Can you put the pizza in the oven when it beeps?" she asked Kaden.

"Sure."

She had a feeling she was going to come back to a partially frozen pizza still sitting on top the stove, but she moved to the small landing outside the front door of her apartment for some privacy. "Hey."

Sprocket curled up behind her when she sat on the top step.

"Hey," Bree said. "What's going on?"

"I have a list," Denise said.

"You have a list? Is there any particular order to your list?" Something crunched over the line.

"Are you eating carrot sticks?" Denise asked.

"Yes. I have exactly twenty-four minutes for lunch today, so you're going to have to deal with me crunching on carrot sticks in your ear while you talk. I'll try to move the microphone away from my mouth while I chew."

"Thanks," she said sarcastically. "No real order, so let me get the big thing out of the way first." She gave Bree an abbreviated version of the previous day, including picking up Kimber and Kaden from school.

"Shit," Bree said.

"Yeah."

"What do you need?"

"Any way we'd be able to move into your house this weekend?"

Crunch. "I haven't officially moved out yet. I mean, most of my personal stuff is at Jase's, but I wasn't sure what you wanted me to leave at my house so I haven't moved any of the big stuff. Jase doesn't have a trip this weekend so he may be able to get some of the guys to help shuffle everything around."

She went over the furniture and rooms she wanted to move and they made plans to meet Saturday morning.

"How's everything else? You sound tired." Bree asked.

Denise sighed. "I'm feeling a little overwhelmed by things. They seem to be piling up at the moment."

"We'll figure it out. What's next? You've got five and a half minutes."

"I think we should get an office manager for the rescue. The paperwork is eating into a lot of my time and I'd rather be working with the dogs than sitting in the office. We can probably get away with someone part-time. Maybe a business major from the college."

"Okay."

"And at least one more full-time person."

"Okay."

"That's it? Okay?"

"With...four minutes left? Yes, that's it. I trust you, Denise. If you're telling me you need more help, I know you need more help. If you need to talk it over more, bring the kids over to Jase's place tonight for dinner. We'll work out a plan of attack and figure out where to advertise for the help."

"Sounds like a plan." Especially if she wouldn't have to figure out what to cook for dinner.

"Anything else?" Bree asked.

"I kind of had sex with Chris again." Why did she throw that in there?

"Oh—Wait. What?"

"I kind of had sex with Chris again?" She cringed this time, waiting for the explosion.

166

"How do you *kind of* have sex with someone? You know what? No. That is the first thing we're talking about tonight. How are you going to drop that on me with less than a minute before I have to get my next patient? You should have started with that."

"We wouldn't have gotten to the rest of what I needed to talk about."

"Beside the point. You getting nookie is the most important topic of discussion."

Denise smiled. "No one calls it nookie anymore, Bree."

"Not the point! Damn it. I have to go. Six o'clock! Heifer."

Bree hung up and Denise grinned at the phone, imagining Bree's frustration at not being able to slam a handset receiver down. There were some advantages to modern technology.

CHAPTER 21

*C*hris braced his hands on the tailgate of his truck, staring at the last two boxes. He remembered those boxes. They were heavy and even though they were the last two, he dreaded picking them up.

Jase returned from his trip into the house, wiping sweat from his brow. Even though it was only early spring, they'd been unloading their trucks and carrying boxes and furniture into his house for well over an hour. "Come on. Last two. They aren't going to walk themselves inside."

"How did we end up doing the brunt of the physical labor?" Somehow the girls had managed to escape while the guys did the heavy lifting. "Isn't this supposed to be the twenty-first century? What happened to women's equality and all that shit?"

Jase laughed. "Why do you think they're in the woods shooting targets while we're doing the manual labor?"

"I'm so confused." Chris slid one of the boxes off the tailgate and hefted it to get a better grip. He wasn't sure what was in it, but if he had to guess, it was a home gym. Or Bree collected bricks. Or kept all her wealth in gold bullion.

"Bree's an Olympic power lifter, right?"

Jase's brow crinkled. "What?"

"That's the only reason I can come up with for how heavy these boxes are."

Jase pulled the last box off the truck with a grunt. "They're probably all books." He looked up at the overcast sky. "Which is why they're in *your* truck, which has a cover, and not mine. The woman would lose her shit if her books got wet in the rain."

"Why does she have eight boxes of encyclopedias?"

Jase grinned. "You know I'm thinking of that *How I Met Your Mother* episode, right?"

"Encyclo-*pae*-dia," they said in unison, then laughed.

His laughter fading, Jase shook his head. "She has hardbacks, paperbacks, reference books. I suggested donating some of them and you'd have thought I'd said we should cut off Charlie's other leg. The woman didn't talk to me for hours. *Hours.*"

"Huh. Good to know. Denise has a lot of books, too." He followed Jase through the front door and into the living room. They stacked the boxes on the floor before the fireplace next to all the other boxes they'd dragged in.

"It's kind of cool though. She's perfectly happy to sit on the couch and read while I'm watching TV. Doesn't care what it is as long as we're on the couch together."

He'd never been the type of guy to get jealous, but damned if he didn't envy what Jase had. Knowing the woman he was with wanted nothing more than to *be* with him. Didn't matter what they were doing or if they were even doing the same thing, just as long as they were together. He wanted that with Denise. Wanted to sit with her on the couch at the end of the day and not worry about why he was there and whether she questioned it, because the only reason he'd be there was because he wanted to be.

"You want a beer?"

"Does the Pope ride in a mobile?" He flopped down on the couch and gratefully took the beer Jase returned with.

"Where's she putting the books?"

Jase sat in the recliner. "I'm adding built-ins along this entire wall." He waved his hand, indicating the brick wall with the large fireplace in the center.

"Wow," Chris said.

"Pretty much." Jase sipped his beer. "You okay, man?"

Chris scrubbed a hand over his head. "Chief wants to send me undercover again."

"How soon?"

"A month if this case isn't wrapped up by then. Sooner if we manage to capture Eddie or get info on how the Anarchists are regrouping."

"Damn."

"Yeah."

"What're you gonna do?"

Wasn't that the question. He had no fucking clue. He didn't want to leave Denise, or the kids, but this was his job. What he'd signed on to do. What he loved...once.

Shit.

He used to live for it. The adrenaline. The rush of doing whatever it took to get the bad guy. Now... Denise smiling at him for making the kids breakfast. Laughing at his look of horror when she suggested he try to do Kimber's hair. He'd never understood how guys could just walk away from the job, but now... Now he knew.

And he didn't know what to do.

"No fucking clue," he said.

"Can I ask you a question?" Jase asked.

Chris frowned. Since when weren't they completely honest with each other? "Yeah, man. Always."

"Why do you still do it?"

"Do what?"

"Go after the target."

He drew a blank. He didn't know how to answer the question.

Jase sat forward in the recliner and rested his elbows on his knees. "I loved it—Special Operations. Being a badass. Following the intel, assessing the objective, and taking down the target. It was a rush. Until I realized it was one huge fucking self-licking ice-cream cone. We weren't making a difference. We weren't even fighting a bad guy. We were fighting a guy who was defending his country—his home. It wasn't anything any of us wouldn't have done if the situation was reversed. I joined the Army to make a difference, but I ended up not liking the difference I made.

"I'm not saying that's the case with you," he continued. "But why do you still do it?"

Chris rubbed his hand over his head, rolling Jase's words over in his mind. "I guess it was the same. Didn't really have a plan when I got out and started college. Figured I take a few classes and figure out what I was going to do with my life. Go into management or something. All those leadership skills I picked up as an NCO," he scoffed.

"This girl I was dating, her little sister went missing. Local cops chalked it up to a runaway, but this girl swore up and down her sister wouldn't run away. They were close and if there was anything going on, she'd have known about it. Her parents took the girl's phone to the local FBI field office and begged them to look it. They found a whole bunch of hidden apps. She'd been lured out, probably trafficked."

He took another drink. "Right in the middle of fucking America. How does that happen? Girl I was seeing dropped out and went back home. I looked into joining the FBI. Had no interest in being a cyber analyst, but special agent? Fuck, yeah. That was right in my wheelhouse. Declared pre-law as my major and the rest is history."

"And now?" Jase asked.

Chris stared into the cold fireplace. "And now, I'm where I was when I got out of the Army. When the Southern Anarchists are gone, another gang will fill the void. The drugs won't stop, the guns won't stop, and families losing their kids won't stop." He looked at Jase. "So what difference am I making?"

"When I started V.E.T. Adventures I just wanted to stop one guy from killing himself the way Tony did. Just one. If I could do that, I'd be a success. The difference we make doesn't have to be huge. Doesn't have to be epic. It can just be one guy." He held up his index finger. "But that guy—he's got a wife. Friends. Parents. Maybe kids. So that one difference can ripple out and affect dozens of people."

"I get it, but why are you telling me this?"

Jase nodded, as if psyching himself up for what he said next. "I'm expanding V.E.T. Adventures. I'm partnering with Denise to pair guys who come through my programs with dogs she has and I got a subcontract with a Veterans Affairs outreach program."

"That's great," Chris said. "Congrats."

"Thanks, but it means more work and more time away from Bree. I've been considering taking on a partner—someone who understands the mission and how important it is. Someone who wants to really make a difference. Normally, I wouldn't have considered asking you, but…things being what they are…"

"What do you mean?"

Jase leaned back in his chair. "Something's off with you. I don't think it's this case, because things were going off before you left. I think you've lost your purpose."

Had he? He was conflicted, that was for sure. He wanted to bring the Anarchists down. Wanted to give his agents' families closure. Stop one more little girl from being taken from her family. But the void they created would be filled by another gang. Maybe one smarter and harder to take down.

"What are you saying?"

Jase pulled at his short beard. "Would you consider coming on as my partner? Not trying to make the decision to transfer harder, but maybe it'd be something you'd consider."

Shock didn't even begin to describe his reaction. Being a

badass door-kicker was pretty much all he'd ever done. It was what he knew. In the Army and the FBI. Could he be satisfied doing a job where all he did was camp and hunt? Hell, he did it a lot in his off-time anyway. He'd seen the change in a couple of guys who went on repeat trips, how the tension and anxiety would lessen over time. Jase made a difference. Maybe not the difference Chris thought he'd make by joining the FBI, but was it more important to stop bad guys from doing bad things or remind good people what they had?

Accepting the offer meant staying. It meant not leaving Denise. It meant lazy weekends together with Kimber and Kaden. The longing for normalcy and Rockwellian bliss was almost debilitating in its intensity.

It also meant giving up the only identity he'd held as an adult.

"When do you need an answer?"

"No rush. Think it over. I can handle things until you know which way you're going to go."

CHAPTER 22

*T*he sharp crack of the rifle echoed off the surrounding trees, sending up a flight of birds that had settled into the branches only minutes before.

"You're still off dead-center by a couple of centimeters," Bree said, sighting the target downrange through binoculars.

Denise raised her head to stare at the target and ejected the spent cartridge from her rifle. "Scope might be off by a hair. I haven't sighted it in almost a year."

Bree turned her head, then peered more over her shoulder. "Could also be that you're kicking your feet up."

Blushing, Denise lowered her feet and splayed them out on the ground in the more traditional prone position. "Habit."

"It still boggles my mind that you made it through the Army while kicking your feet up when you shoot."

Denise made the adjustments to the scope and pressed her cheek against the rifle stock. She sighted through the crosshairs and focused on her breathing and the beat of her heart. The thin lines of the optics rose and fell with each breath. She paused at the end of the inhale, counted to three and exhaled. At the bottom of the breath, she again paused and counted, squeezing the trigger until she felt the slight resistance in her finger, and fired when she hit three.

"Dead center," Bree said. She glanced over her shoulder and grinned. "Guess it was the scope."

Denise dropped her head and kicked her feet, which had come up again at some point. She raised her head. "That's how I got through the Army with kicking my feet up. I always shot expert."

"How did your dad let you get away with it?"

She smiled and laughed. "My mom told him it was cute and to leave me alone. That was the first time I remember seeing his eye twitch. He said, 'Karen. There is nothing cute about being able to take out a target at two-hundred meters.' She threatened to dress me in a tutu the next time he took me hunting just to prove there was. This was way before they made pink camo, otherwise I'd have been hunting in that."

"I can totally hear your parents having that argument." Bree glanced at her watch, then up at the sky. "We've got about fifteen more minutes before we lose all the good light. Thank goodness the rain held off today."

While packing up the rest of her bedroom at the rescue, she'd pulled out her rifle from under the bed where it had been collecting dust and realized she hadn't been shooting since before Sarah got sick. Her off-handed comment had led to Bree's suggestion that they get some target practice in before the sun set.

She'd jumped at the chance. For some reason, she'd always found shooting targets relaxing. The rhythm, the focus, the precision—it all calmed her. She had no choice but to let go of everything when she was shooting, otherwise she couldn't focus on the hitting the target. Even in the heat of battle, she'd been able to keep her cool by focusing on the mechanics.

She'd set up to take another shot when Bree asked, "So what's going on with you and Chris?"

She jerked the trigger and the shot went wide, hitting the edge of the target. She raised her head from the rifle and turned it slowly, glaring at Bree through slitted eyes.

Bree's face was the definition of feigned innocence. "Was it something I said?"

"You're lucky I like you."

"I know, right? Spill. I watched you with him today. You were this weird combination of standoffish and blushing school girl."

Laying the rifle down, she rubbed her eyes. "I'm not sure I know what I want."

"Yes, you do," Bree said. "You're just afraid to admit it."

Denise stacked her hands and rested her chin on them. "I want what you and Jase have," she said quietly, turning her head toward Bree.

"What's stopping you?"

"When we're together, it's great. I'm in the moment and I can pretty much ignore all the other crap, but when we're apart…"

"When you're apart you question whether it's real or if it's the adrenaline or the situation or just horniness."

Denise pressed her lips together. "Yeah. How did you figure out it was real?"

"I listened to you." Bree smiled.

"What the hell did you do that for?"

"It made sense at the time."

"And now?"

"And now I think you should listen to your own advice."

"I don't think I could take it if he walked away again." The bottom dropped out of her stomach at the mere thought of giving him another chance and him choosing his job over her. "If I go all in and it doesn't work, what then?"

Bree rested her head on her hands and mirrored Denise's position. "Not every relationship works. You run that risk no matter what. But you have to give it the chance to work first. If you go in from the very beginning with the idea that it's going to fail, then you're doomed before you even start."

"It's hard not to think the current circumstances are driving our relationship right now."

Bree raised her eyebrows. "So you admit you have a relationship?"

"We have...something. It's not like we can do normal relationship stuff."

"Like what?"

"Like go on a date," she said.

"Do you want to go on a date?"

"Kind of," she admitted.

"Then ask him on a date," Bree said.

"Just like that?"

"Sure. Why not?"

"I don't think it's the right time with everything going on at the moment."

Bree raised her head and rested her chin in her hand. "That's just an excuse. Kimber and Kaden are with your parents until tomorrow night. Now's the perfect time to go on a date. You don't have to worry about a sitter, which I would totally be willing to do, by the way, and you can pick what you do."

Denise rose onto her elbows and picked the cuticle of her thumb. He had already kind of asked her out. Hell, he'd even asked her dad for permission to date her. All she was really doing was setting the date.

But that meant putting herself out there and opening herself up to the possibility of being rejected and hurt. Maybe not immediately, but a few weeks or months down the road when he left again. Could she deal with that? The twisting feeling in the center of her chest told her she'd have a really, really hard time with it. This thing with Chris, whatever it was, felt big. Important. It loomed around the edges of her life and she knew if she let down her walls it would overwhelm and consume her.

What she really had to decide was whether that would be the worst thing in the world.

She nodded a couple of times. "Okay."

"Okay?"

She looked at Bree. "Why do you sound so surprised?"

"I thought for sure it was going to take more convincing than that. I didn't even have to pull out any Disney quotes. I'm kind of bummed."

Denise grinned. "You're a dork."

"You love me."

They heard an engine coming down the hard-packed dirt lane and they both turned to look.

"Speak of the devil," Bree said.

Denise shifted her weight and picked up the rifle, holding it out to Bree. "Here. There's five rounds left. May as well shoot them while we have the last bit of light."

She took the binoculars and adjusted the focus as she stared through them at the target. Bree shot the last few rounds in quick succession, forming a small grouping below the main target. She lowered the binoculars and smirked.

"You mad at Jase about something?"

Bree grinned. "No. I just like to keep him on his toes." She rose to her knees and cleared the rifle before handing it back to Denise.

Denise pushed up to her knees as well. "I don't think it's his toes Jase is going to worry about."

Bree raised her eyebrows and smirked, then headed toward the truck and Jase.

Even without the crunch of footsteps, Denise would have known Chris was close behind her. It was the cheesiest thing in the world but she could feel his presence.

He squatted down next to her, balancing on his toes and picked up the binoculars. "Nice grouping," he said. "Who shot off the poor dude's penis?"

"That would be Bree," she said. "Her humor can be a little twisted sometimes."

"Remind me not to piss her off."

"I think it should go without saying you shouldn't piss any woman off." She stood, cradling the rifle in her arms. "What have you guys been doing?"

He rose as well. "Sitting around with our hands in our pants. You know. Guy stuff."

She grinned. No doubt they'd both fallen asleep watching some game on TV. "What are you doing later?"

"Don't have anything planned. Why?"

She dropped her gaze to the vee of his green t-shirt. "Would you like to get dinner?"

"No."

She exhaled sharply, her heart plummeting. She nodded, not trusting her voice to say anything.

He tilted her chin up, forcing her to look at him. "You're not stealing my thunder, Denise. I'm doing the asking. I've already got something in mind for tomorrow—if you're free."

Pressing her lips together to keep the stupid, sappy grin from breaking free, she nodded again. "Other than unpacking, I don't have anything going on."

"Can you give me a lift back to my truck?"

She shrugged, more than a little disappointed that he didn't want to take advantage of Kimber and Kaden spending the night with her parents. "Sure. Where is it?"

"Jase's house."

Her brows pinched together. "Yeah, sure."

"I need to get my jacket from your house, too."

"My house at the rescue? My house as in Sarah's house? Or my house as in Bree's house?"

He chuckled low, the rumble sending a shiver coursing down her back. "You have a lot of houses. Are you going to remember where you need to go tomorrow?"

"I don't know. It may take me a couple of days before I figure it out."

"Bree's house." He tucked a small strand of hair behind her ear. "I took it off when we started moving all the books on our last trip."

"Okay."

He shoved his hand into the pocket of his cargo pants, pushing them dangerously lower. "And I was hoping I could convince you to feed me."

"You smelled the chicken." She'd taken the slow-cooker over the day before and asked Bree to set it up so she wouldn't have to worry about scrounging for food after moving all day.

"I smelled the chicken." He stepped closer. "I'm willing to make a trade for some of that spicy chicken," he said next to her ear.

A nervous flutter spread from her belly. Chris would be at her house. With no kids and a bed nearby. "Hmm. I'm sure we can work something out. I have a lot of boxes to unpack."

"You do, huh?"

"Tons of boxes. It'll probably take all night."

"Guess it's a good thing I brought an overnight bag then."

"Guess it is." She winked and stepped around him to put her rifle in its case. With her back to him, she finally let the goofy smile lose.

She had a date.

"I'm so close," she whispered. Her head fell back as one of Chris's hands moved down the center of her body, from her neck to where she sat astride him. Her hips rolled as she rose and fell, his thick erection buried impossibly deep.

"That's it, Denise. Fuck yeah. Squeeze me tighter, baby." He rubbed his thumb between her folds, wetting it then rubbing the hood of her clit.

"Oh, fuck." Looking down at him, she braced her hands on his chest. That sweet tension gathered in her core like flood waters behind a dam, ready to burst.

He bit his lower lip and thrust up with his hips. "Christ, Denise. I'm holding back as best I can. I want you to come."

She took his thumb and moved it millimeters to the left. "Right there."

"What do you need?"

"Small circles. Hard. Fast," she told him. "There. Right there. Oh, God." Her head fell back again and she jerked her hips faster as she came, an explosion of starbursts behind her eyes following the pulse coursing through her body.

He flipped her onto her back, stealing her breath. Hooking his arms under her knees, he spread her wide and drove into her. He buried himself deep and his whole body shuddered. Unhooking his arms, he wrapped her legs around his hips and continued to thrust. Softer now that he'd come, but no less intense.

Turning his head, he nipped her neck. Shivers shot down her body and she groaned.

"Unless you can go again, you need to stop doing that," she said.

He stilled. "I'm pretty sure I'm dead. There's no going again for a while."

She smiled and ran her hands up his back. "That's what I figured."

He rubbed the bridge of his nose along her jawline, then kissed her briefly. "Be right back."

"'Kay." Waiting until he'd gone into the bathroom and shut the door, Denise grabbed her robe from the hook on the closet door and used the kids' bath in the hall to clean up then fixed two glasses of water.

Chris was asleep on his back, his chest rising and falling evenly when she returned. He'd pulled the sheet up only to his waist.

Setting one of the glasses on the table next to him, she took a moment to admire all the glorious muscles and tattoos on display in her bed. It was definitely something she could let herself get used to.

She threw the robe on the end of the bed and lay down on her side in her normal position, facing away from Chris. It felt weird to cuddle up next to him while he was asleep. Plus, she wasn't much of a cuddler.

In that moment between being fully awake and asleep, he rolled over and pulled her back into his front, jarring her awake again. Her arms shot out and her whole body jerked at the movement.

"Shh. 'S okay, baby. I gotch you."

Her heart thundered in her chest. Not only from how abruptly she woke, but also from what he said. She could tell from his slurred words that he wasn't fully awake. They said the most honest people were drunks and kids, but people on the edge of sleep fell into that category. One reason they used sleep deprivation as an interrogation technique.

It was such a simple statement, but it said so much.

She adjusted her head on the pillow and wiggled into his embrace. She could learn to be a cuddler. Her eyelids eased closed, a small smile on her lips.

"I want you to be my person," he mumbled.

Her eyes snapped open and stayed that way for a long time.

CHAPTER 23

"Hey, Denise?" Nick, one of her employees, called from the reception door.

"Yeah?" She closed the kennel door and took the leash to hang up on the pegs along the wall.

"I just got a call from the county shelter that there's an abandoned dog. They think it might have been hit by a car. They're full."

Shit. That was their code for "the dog will be euthanized if we get it." She glanced at the clock. There was no way she'd have time to go get a dog, bring it back here, and make it home in time to meet the school bus.

Damn it. She closed her eyes and rubbed her forehead. They needed to hire more people. She'd cut back on her afternoon hours to be home for Kimber and Kaden, but everything in the rescue was starting to back up.

"Do you need me to go get it?"

She dropped her hands. "You'd do that?"

Nick pushed through the door and walked toward her. "Sure, why not?"

"It's not something you normally do."

He shrugged and crossed his arms. "It's true, you've always picked up any dogs we get calls for, but you also lived here and had no life."

"I'm sorry I haven't been around as much."

"You've got a family now. They should be your priority."

"You don't mind?" she asked.

"Not at all. Should I bring it back here or straight to Doc Abbie?"

Normally, she made that call, but it was time she release the stranglehold she had on every facet of her life. "Make the call when you see the dog."

He stood up straighter. "Really?"

Jeez, had she really been that much of a control freak? "Yeah. I trust your judgment. Just call Doc Abbie's office first so they know you're coming."

"Wow. Yeah. I will. Is there anything special I should take?"

She helped him pack a kit with the equipment she normally took with her on pick-ups. After he left, she looked through the appointment schedule to see whether anyone needed to be rescheduled. It meant more back-to-back appointments the rest of the week, but it couldn't be helped.

Note to self: look through all the office manager applications tonight.

Rubbing the center of her forehead again, she sighed. She'd work with a couple of the dogs she absolutely had to, clean the kennels, feed everyone, and hopefully get out of there on time.

After rescheduling her clients, she glanced down at Sprocket. "You staying here or coming with me to the barn?"

The dog raised her head, groaned, and laid it back down again.

"I don't think so." She bent and patted her on the side, scratching the base of her tail for good measure. "You've done nothing all day but lay around. You can walk your lazy butt over to the barn with me and lay down over there. Come on."

Sprocket lumbered to her feet, a low whine protesting the effort.

"Whatever."

Her phone pinged as they crossed the yard.

Chris: Busy?

That's rhetorical, right?

A few seconds later, her phone rang, Chris's name flashing across the screen.

"So, that's a yes?"

"Yeah, that's a yes."

"What's going on?"

She lifted the latch on the barn door and stepped through, leaving it open for Sprocket to follow.

"Well, Nick had to go get a dog so I had to reschedule all my afternoon appointments so I can take care of everything and still get out of here in time to pick up the kids." She tucked the phone into her shoulder to grab the stack of metal food bowls in what used to be the tack room, now used to store food and equipment.

"Who else is there?" Chris asked.

"Just me."

Sprocket began barking from the main area of the barn. Denise turned in that direction as if she could see through the wall at what had set her off.

"What do you mean, just you?" Chris asked.

The phone beeped in her ear. *For fuck's sake.* She pulled it away to see who was calling.

"Hang on, the school is calling."

"Denise—"

She switched lines. "Hello?"

"Hello. Ms. Reynolds?"

"Yes."

"This is Alicia from the front office of Springer Elementary."

The barking had grown louder with several other dogs joining

Sprocket and she closed the door to the tack room. She'd find out what set them off after the call.

"Yes?" An acrid smell permeated the air and she twitched her nose to get rid of the itch it caused. *What is that?*

"We'd like to know if Kimber and Kaden will be returning to school after their dental appointment."

Her gut contracted. "What do you mean return to school? They should be at school now."

"No, ma'am. Their father signed them out for their dental appointment before lunch."

She dropped the bowls, the clatter of them hitting the concrete floor adding to the cacophony of the dogs' barking.

"There's a no-contact court order against their father, who is a wanted felon, so would you mind explaining to me how the fuck he signed them out of school?" she shouted.

No. No. No. This is not happening. Adrenaline and a heavy dose of fear coursed through her.

"I—"

"Fuck!" Her skin tightened as goose bumps rose from every pore of her body. Her vision narrowed, then expanded.

She switched back to Chris and wrenched open the tack room door.

"Chris—" Smoke billowed around her and she coughed as it wrapped around her head.

Every dog was barking or howling. Sprocket stood in front of the now closed barn door, snarling and barking.

"Denise!"

"I'm here. He took the kids. The barn's on fire."

Thick, black, oily smoke billowed up from the bottom of the door. Flames danced and crackled within the smoke, reaching halfway up the wall. A quick glance at the other end of the barn showed a similar situation, although the fire hadn't progressed as much.

That old barn's probably got some really dry wood.

Fucking Eddie.

No fire or smoke was visible from the sides of the barn. Probably because the chain link enclosures kept out whatever asshole had started the fire.

"Where are you?" Chris asked.

"In the barn. Sprocket, come." Hackles raised and a snarl still played at her mouth but the dog obeyed.

"Fucking hell."

"Pretty much." She went back into the tack room.

"Why are you so calm?"

She tossed storage containers off the shelf, looking for the one that held the promotional merchandise. "Would you rather I be hysterical, suck in a bunch of smoke, and pass out? I don't really have time for that right now."

"Son of a bitch. I'm fifteen minutes away."

"How are you fifteen minutes away?" In a shoe box-sized container she found the *I heart Wiggle Butts* bandanas she'd had made for an adoption event and grabbed two.

"I was already on my way. Fire department is on the way as well and I've got a team working on the kids."

He must have radioed it in. At least that was one less thing she had to do.

"Gotta go. Gotta get the dogs out of the barn."

"Get yourself out, Denise." His voice was strained and rose at the end, as if he was suppressing his desire to shout at her.

"Yup. That, too." She ended the call and jammed the phone into her back pocket. Wetting the bandana in the utility sink, she tied one around her hair and one around her face. Some goggles would have been nice, but all she had were shooting glasses and those wouldn't stop the smoke from reaching her eyes.

She considered using the water hose to wet down the doors, but the color and thickness of the smoke made her think they'd doused the wood with some kind of fuel. Pouring water on it would only spread it faster.

She needed to get the dogs closest to the fire out first. Opening the door to the first stall, she shoved the small pit bull mix away from the dog door leading to the enclosed outside pen. The frantic dog was trying to dig its way out through the concrete floor.

Lifting the hasp, she slid the bolt back. The dog ran out into the pen when she threw the door wide. If she could—

A crack rent the air, followed by a sharp bark and whimper.

No. No. No. She took a step back and bent at the waist to look out the small door. The dog lay on its side, a dark spot growing on its hip.

Motherfucker shot one of her dogs.

"God damn it!"

She stood and laced her hands on top of her head. Panic loomed, threatening to steal her breath and her resolve.

Think, Reynolds. Think.

Turning in a circle she looked for another way out. She had to get the dogs and herself out safely, but to do that she had to remove the threat outside. Closing her eyes, she dropped her head back. Sprocket lay down on her feet and whined. Whether from the smoke or from the defeat that crept around the edges of her mind, tears formed in the corners of her eyes.

She snapped them open and stared at the empty hayloft above her.

Higher ground.

Dogs first. She hurried to open all the stall doors. Some of the dogs burst out and milled around in the center of the barn while others cowered in the corners of their stalls. She didn't have time to coax them out.

A vertical wooden ladder led up to one of the haylofts that ran the length of both sides of the barn. If there was more than one person out there, they'd be set up on either side of the building, waiting for her try to escape. Maybe they thought the dog had been her. Maybe it was a warning. If it was only one shooter, they'd probably circle around, assuming she'd try the other side.

She paused halfway up the ladder and glanced over her shoulder at the matching ladder across the aisle. Unless they thought she'd assume that and would try again on the same side, instead of crossing over.

Sprocket barked at her from the base of the ladder.

"You're right." She climbed the last few rungs. "They aren't that smart."

Stepping onto the loft's plywood platform, she moved directly to the closest of four large windows. Most of them had been replaced when they refurbished the barn and they'd opted for wooden doors instead of glass.

Pulling her Glock from the low-profile holster, she lifted the window latch up, careful not to let the door swing open. Opening it enough to scan the area around the barn, she couldn't see anyone near the end of the barn.

Would they expect her to try the middle of the barn, away from the fires?

She closed the window and latched it, moving to the second window. Easing it open, she crouched to the side to get a better view. Dark smoke filled the air and she could feel the heat at her back as the flames climbed higher.

She was running out of time.

Glancing at the other side of the building, she almost missed the guy in black with a rifle move from behind a tree at the edge of the field.

She dropped to a knee and her supporting foot kept the door from swinging open. He ran across the field, making no effort to hide his movements. Either he wasn't worried about getting caught or he was getting the hell out of dodge.

Adjusting for elevation to hit center mass, she inhaled and paused, fighting the cough that threatened. She paused again at the bottom of her exhale and squeezed the trigger. A coughing fit overtook her, but she kept her gun aimed at the man she'd just shot.

She counted ten very long seconds to see if he would move before dashing to the ladder. Holstering her weapon, she slid most of the way down, wincing as the splinters dug into her palm.

Sprocket sat at the bottom of the ladder, howling.

Denise ran to the tack room and grabbed a set of bolt cutters plus several leashes from hooks on a wall. Racing back to the center stall on the same side she'd fired from, she tried to herd as many dogs as possible into the stall.

She threw open the dog door and several attempted to squeeze through at once. Palming her gun again, she shoved two out of the way and took her chances as she crawled through the opening, pulling the cutters and leashes with her. Staying on a knee, she raised her Glock and scanned the area.

Nothing, and no one, moved. She holstered her gun, draped the leashes around her neck, and picked up the cutters. Duck walking to the back fence, she cut the horizontal retaining wires in the chain link. Dropping the cutters, she clipped two leashes to the bottom of the fence, threw the ends over the top bar and used it as a pulley to lift the bottom of the fence, creating an opening for the dogs.

Once one dog realized there was a way out, they all spilled through, almost knocking her to her ass in the process. She tied off the leashes to make sure the fence remained open.

She glanced toward where the body was and back at the barn. Damn it. She needed to make sure all the dogs were out. Taking a bracing breath, she crawled back into the barn. Three dogs had to be picked up and carried to the escape route stall and shoved through the door and she earned a few bites for her efforts.

Crawling through after the last dog, she stayed on all fours, panting for breath. Sprocket licked her face and head-butted her shoulder, urging her to move. The faint wail of sirens reached her and she pushed to her feet. There was one more thing she needed to do before the cavalry arrived.

She low crawled under the fence and pushed back to her feet, stumbling toward the body in the field.

If he was still alive, he was going to wish he'd died from the gunshot.

Because she still had to find her kids.

CHAPTER 24

*T*he last of the police and the ambulance finally left with an admonishment that Denise shouldn't refuse treatment. She'd sucked on the oxygen mask enough to help with the residual cough from the fire, but she needed to finish checking on the dogs and the guy she had trussed up in the storage room next to her office.

Hopefully, he hadn't bled out. She'd stuffed some cloth in the wound, but hadn't had time for more extensive first aid before the fire trucks and police had shown up.

Chris sat down next to her on the steps up to her old apartment. "I think you should go to the hospital."

And she needed to get rid of Chris.

"I'm fine," she said.

"You're not."

She turned her head. "You're right, I'm not. But unless you're going to tell me Kaden and Kimber are there waiting for me, going to the hospital isn't going to make me better."

"Denise—"

Fisting her hands, she closed her eyes and exhaled through her teeth. "Find. Them."

"We're working on it. Our team is going through all the cameras around the school, tracking where he went after he took them. There's a BOLO out for the vehicle and an Amber Alert for the kids."

She pressed the heels of her hands into her eyes. "I need to check on the dogs. I have to stay busy or I'm going to go crazy."

"Do you want help?"

"No." Her answer was short, even to her. She took a breath. "Please find them."

He pressed a kiss again her temple. "I'll keep you updated."

Nodding, she watched him go to his truck and lifted her hand in response to his wave, then followed his progress until he turned out of the drive.

Too much time had been wasted dealing with the fire and answering questions from the police and the FBI. She doubled over, her forehead to her knees, when the sob tore through her. It was happening again. Only now was a thousand times worse. She'd promised them—promised Sarah—she'd keep them safe and that bastard had taken them.

Were they scared? Was he hurting them? Not knowing was the worst kind of torture. She needed to find out where they were.

Her rage was a palpable thing that she needed to get under control, but it seethed beneath her skin and flowed like lava through her veins. She could only hope she had enough control not to kill the guy before she could get the information she needed.

Heading into the kennel, she was assailed by barks, howls, and whines from the dogs she'd moved in after rounding them up outside. The noise would help drown out any screams that might otherwise be heard by the firefighters still working on the barn. Sprocket met her at the entrance and followed her to the storage room.

A twinge of doubt unfurled as she paused with her hand on the knob. She squatted down and buried her face in Sprocket's nape.

Should she have told Chris about the guy? Let him take this asshole for official questioning? She shook her head. No. He'd lawyer up and her chance to get answers would be gone.

Despite the inferno burning inside her and the tears she couldn't stop pouring down her face, she was calm. She knew exactly what needed to be done.

Anything to save her kids.

Giving Sprocket one last hug, she stood and opened the door. Using her foot to keep Sprocket out, she closed the door softly behind her. The guy was awake and glaring at her. She'd give him one chance. "Where are they? Please. They're just little kids," Denise implored.

"Fuckin' seriously? You think some weak-ass tears are gonna get me to talk? You ain't never seein' those brats again. Fuckin' bitch." He tried to pull off an air of superiority. He thought because she was a woman and was crying, he had nothing to worry about.

She laughed and walked to the small workbench, bending to pull out an old metal tool box she kept there. "You made a lot of mistakes today, Jeffrey." She glanced at him and saw him flinch when she used his name.

"I pilfered your wallet while I was searching you for weapons." She flipped open the rusty clasp locks and lifted the lid. Rummaging through the contents, she kept her tone conversational.

"Of course, information is a kind of weapon. Cute kids, by the way."

A low growl emanated from him. She pocketed a screwdriver and a pair of pliers, then hefted a ball peen hammer in her hand before turning around.

"Lucky for you, I don't consider kids to be a weapon." She pointed the hammer at him and cocked her head. "Unlike some people.

"Your first mistake, Jeff, was taking my kids at all." She walked behind him, trailing the fingers of her free hand up his arm and over his shoulder. "Then you set fire to my barn and shot one of my dogs."

She continued around behind him, keeping her touch light, almost like a caress. "But your biggest mistake was thinking my tears are a sign of weakness." From behind, she dug her fingers into the wound she'd half-heartedly bandaged.

He grunted and let out a low, teeth-clenched scream and his fists clenched and unclenched.

"But you see, my tears are kind of like a release valve on a pressure cooker." She leaned forward so her mouth was close to his ear. "The rage needs somewhere to go," she whispered. "I have to let it out somehow because you have to tell me things. Things I need to know. Things you need to be alive to tell me and if I don't let the rage out somehow, I'm going to bash your fucking skull in before you tell me where my kids are." She kissed his cheek before pulling back. "So don't ever think my tears are a sign of weakness."

Denise rounded the front of the chair, the hammer in her hand. "That was your only chance for me to ask nicely. Every time you refuse to tell me where they are, I will hurt you."

Please just tell me where they are. She didn't want to be back in this place. Threatening and seducing answers from a detainee. If he would just tell her they could both—

"Keep fucking crying, bitch," Jeffrey said.

The door on getting out of there easily slammed shut and a terrible calm descended through her. She inhaled, twirled the hammer in her hand, and swung it forcefully down onto his right wrist, eliciting a shrill scream.

Denise slid the hammer into the back pocket of her jeans. She leaned down and grasped his wrists, squeezing his forearm and forcing the broken bones together. He responded with a sobbing grunt.

"Weak. Fucking. Cunt," he said through clenched teeth.

Denise sighed and stood up. "Oh, Jeffrey. That mistake is going to be a painful one. I know how to keep you in an excruciating amount of pain. I was trained by the best. Or the worst, depending on how you want to look at it."

"You think my club is going to let you get away with this? Doesn't matter if you get your brats back or not, you're dead." He turned his head to follow her as she circled around him again.

Ignoring his threat, she rested her elbows on his shoulders. "That was your throttle hand. It's going to be incredibly difficult to ride a motorcycle with a shattered wrist. It may never heal right." She pressed down, putting pressure on the wound in his shoulder. "Tell me where my kids are."

"Fuck. You."

She gave him credit for holding out. He reeked of fear and sweat beaded on his forehead.

"Do you know where the phrase, "so scared I shit my pants" comes from? No? See, it's tied to the body's fight-or-flight response. Your brain will start diverting all efforts to that response and will cause your body to shut down non-essential functions. Like pissing and shitting. You'll get to that point eventually." She released the pressure from his shoulders. "Everyone does."

Fucking with his head would get him to share the information as fast as the physical pain she was going to put him through. In most circumstances it was more effective than physical torture, but she didn't have that kind of time to dedicate to getting what she needed.

Swinging the hammer from behind, she brought it down on his other wrist. That time he cried out.

"Every time you refuse to tell me where my kids are, I'm going to hurt you," she said. "It may be something small. It may be some-thing big. Either way, I'm going to keep you alive while maxi-mizing the pain. Where are my kids?"

"Suck my dick," he managed to grit out.

Sighing, she dropped the hammer and rounded the front of the chair, kneeling on the dick he'd told her to suck, pushing all her weight through her knee. "Gonna be kind of hard to do that when I rip it out by the root, Jeffrey. Bet my dogs would love it though. I wonder what it would be like to watch your own dick be chopped up into dog food. Of course, not being a guy, it's hard for me to process that image."

She lifted the back of her shirt and pulled out her gun, pressing it against the top of his knee. "But first, do you know what a nine millimeter bullet will do to a kneecap at point blank range? Me neither, but I'm willing to find out in three...two..."

"Alright! Alright! They're at Eddie's mom's house in Fayetteville."

"Address."

He rattled off the address and she removed her knee and the gun. She patted him on the cheek. "Don't go anywhere, Jeff. I'll be back if you're lying to me."

Closing the door behind her, she leaned against it and sank to the floor. Sprocket was on her immediately, snout in her neck. Denise wrapped her arms around the dog and sobbed into her fur. Sprocket licked the side of her face and whined. Pulling away from the warm tongue, she wiped away her tears. Someone had to go get Kimber and Kaden.

She pulled her phone out of her back pocket and dialed Chris's number.

He answered on the second ring. "Everything okay?"

"They're at Eddie's mom's house," she said.

"How do you know that?"

"I can't answer that question."

Silence for several seconds. "Do you know the address?"

She told him the address Jeffrey had given her and heard him speaking to someone else.

"Alright. We're checking it out. I'll call you back."

"Okay. Thanks."

"Denise."

"Yeah?"

"Do you need help? With how you got that information?"

This couldn't touch him. There was no good way out of that scenario for either of them. He'd either be forced to arrest her or compromise his principles and put his job at risk.

"No."

"You can trust me, Denise. Whatever it is."

She squeezed her eyes closed and dropped her head against the door. "I do trust you. It isn't about that."

"Then what is it?"

"It's about you having a job to do and not being distracted. Get Kaden and Kimber and call me when you have them."

Disconnecting, she switched to the keypad and dialed Graham's number.

"Hello?"

"I need help with something," she said.

"Fuck, Denise. I'm on it. We're going through footage from around the school. We'll find them."

"I already found out where they are."

"How did you do that?"

"That's what I need help with."

"Does Nolton know?"

She scratched Sprocket's ear. "I told him where the kids are, not how I knew."

"Where are you?"

"The rescue."

"Give me thirty."

"Park in the back. The fire department is still here."

THE ONLY THING keeping her mind off Kaden and Kimber was caring for the dogs, which led to thoughts of how much they had lost, and how much it was going to cost to rebuild. Moving around prevented her from shaking with fury. Poor Sprocket finally lay down in front of the storage room door and watched her walk back and forth.

Needing to stay busy, Denise fed the dogs she'd managed to herd inside. Some of them she'd been able to double up in the larger kennels, but there were still several that had to be put into airline crates. At least they'd calmed down to the point that only a few whined every now and then.

"Denise?"

She closed the kennel door and stood. "In the back," she called.

Graham pushed through the swinging door, followed by a woman. There was something familiar about her and she scanned her from head to toe. The bracelet tattoo caught her attention and recognition struck.

"Paige?"

"Hey," she said with a wave.

"Holy shit. Where did you come from?" In three quick strides, Denise hugged the woman who'd been her trailer-mate at one time on deployment.

She laughed softly and returned the hug. "Savannah for about the last three years."

"How did you end up with Graham?" Denise glanced between the two of them.

Paige shrugged. "I was getting out. He said 'come work for me.' He offered me an obscene amount of money and I had nothing better to do at the time."

Denise nodded, trying to picture the nervous, inexperienced girl she'd known with the confident woman in front of her. No telling what kind of thoughts she was having about Denise.

"What's the situation you need help with?" Graham asked.

She cocked her head toward the back of the building and led the way.

"Did you lose any dogs?" he asked.

"Not to the fire. A couple took off when we got out of the barn."

He stopped her with a hand on her arm. "What do you mean when *we* got out of the barn?"

"I was in the barn when the fire was set."

His eyes narrowed to a squinty glare she recognized. He pointed at the door. "This part of that issue as well?"

Denise pursed her lips and looked at the door.

Paige leaned close. "I think you should have saved that piece of information for later," she said in a stage whisper. "He's already pissed off one of our guys lost the kids."

She snapped her head around. "What do you mean one of your guys lost the kids?"

Paige leaned back, glanced at Graham, then back at Denise. "Shit. We had a guy watching the school. He got run off by the neighborhood watch around the same time Eddie Perry showed up at the school."

Denise closed her eyes and took a deep breath. It was no use getting angry. She couldn't change the past, but would it be too much for life to have given her five fucking minutes? That's all it would have taken for Graham's guy to realize what was going on. Pressing her lips together she opened the door to the storeroom.

Graham went in and stopped, looking down at the guy slumped down in the chair. His chest rose and fell, so he'd either passed out from the pain or had simply fallen asleep.

"Hammer?" Graham asked.

"Ball peen."

Graham reached for the guy's collar and pulled it away from the side of his neck, revealing the top of a gray and black tattoo.

"He's Rebel Yell, not SA," he said as he stood.

Denise shook her head. "What's that?"

"They're another motorcycle club. Except for some minor infractions, they're a bunch of good ol' boys who like to ride and get a little rowdy. There's a faction that wants to take a more profitable, but illegal, route. Didn't know any of them were working with the SA's though."

"How do you know that if they're local?"

"It was started by a former Army guy. There's a few chapters around other bases, including Hunter."

There was more to his story, but before she could ask her phone rang and she pulled it out of her pocket. Chris's name flashed across the screen.

"Go on. We'll take care of this." He pointed at Jeffrey.

Denise stared at Graham, then at the guy she'd tortured. She pulled her bottom lip between her teeth, then looked at her phone as it stopped ringing.

"We're not going to kill him, Denise," Graham said. "We don't do that kind of clean up. Honestly if you were anyone else, we wouldn't do this."

"What are you going to do then?" She didn't want his death on her hands, but at the same time she didn't want to be constantly looking over her shoulder for another attack.

"We'll drop him off at the local Rebel Yell chapter house with a note tying him to the Southern Anarchists. His people will take care of him. How they do that, will be up to them."

"We'll do our best to make sure it doesn't come back to you," Paige said.

Her phone rang again.

"Go," Paige said. "I'll send you my information. If you need anything, let me know." She tilted her head. "I missed you."

Denise hugged Paige. "I missed you, too," she whispered.

Paige squeezed her eyes closed and rubbed Denise's back. "Get out of here. We've got this."

CHAPTER 25

*C*hris jogged behind the three guys in front of him, his M-4 at the low ready. He'd conceded the point position, but he wasn't about to let the team go in without him. Small team tactics might not be his bread and butter anymore, but he still knew what the hell he was doing.

He'd promised Denise he was going to get Kaden and Kimber and he was damn well going to deliver.

Taking up position to the right of the door, he knelt behind the other team member, ready to cover his back when they broke down the door. There would be no polite knocking.

"FBI!" the breacher shouted before slamming the metal battering ram into the door.

The door splintered and swung open as the agent stepped aside to allow the point man in. Chris was through the door in seconds, weapon at the ready as he swept to the right.

"On the ground! On the ground!" An agent had an older woman on her stomach in front of the couch, a bag of chips strewn on the floor in front of her.

He ignored her shouts that they couldn't do this. The hell they couldn't. The adrenaline had begun to kick in and his pulse pounded in his ears, making the chatter of information difficult to hear. He fought to keep his breathing steady as he followed the point man down the short hall to the bedrooms.

"I have the left."

"Copy," he said. "I have the right." Putting his back to the wall, he opened the door with his left hand, pushing hard so it would hit the wall. He swung his weapon into the doorway and swept the room. With no one visible in the room, he approached the accordion closet doors from the side and pushed one open, then the other.

"Clear," he said into his throat mic.

"Clear."

Reentering the hallway, he took the lead and indicated the room on the left. He pushed the door open and repeated the clearing procedure in the empty room.

Two shots rang out behind him and he spun, rifle pressed to his cheek. Eddie Perry lay in the doorway. Another agent approached and kicked the gun out of his hand, before flipping him to his stomach and cuffing his hands behind his back. Chris could tell from the limpness of his body it was a wasted effort.

"Target down," the agent said. He then moved into the other room and returned quickly, shaking his head.

Chris's heart squeezed. Fuck. Where were the kids?

Think. Where would he be if he were a scared kid? Crouching down, he looked under the bed. Christ, he wouldn't have crawled under there, no matter how scared he was.

A small whimper came from the closet. He hung his head. The gunshots had distracted him from checking the closet. Turning his head, he looked at the closed doors.

"Kaden. Kimber," he said softly. "It's Chris. I'm going to open the doors, okay? Don't be afraid."

He duck-walked three steps to the closet and eased the doors apart. Kaden had curled himself around Kimber to protect her as best he could and had his hand over her mouth to stifle her crying. Her tear-filled eyes looked bigger than usual over the palm of his hand.

Chris swallowed hard. "Hey, guys. It's okay. I'm here to take you home."

"Where's Aunt Denise?" Kaden asked.

"She's waiting for you. But we need to get you out of here. Can I carry you?"

Kimber nodded and pulled Kaden's hand away from her mouth. "I want to go home."

Chris glanced over his shoulder for a blanket or sheet. They didn't need the extra trauma of seeing Eddie's body in the hall. He stood and pulled the knit blanket from the bed, throwing it over his shoulder. Beckoning them out of the closet, he squatted down and picked them up, one in each arm.

Grunting, he said, "Oh my gosh, you two are heavy." Kimber buried her face in his neck, but he wanted to be sure neither of them saw anything. "Can you pull the blanket over your heads? I want to protect you from all the lights outside. It's going to hurt your eyes after being in the dark closet." That was partially true. There were probably a lot of police and medical vehicles outside by now, in addition to the news vans that managed to show up like scavengers on a carcass.

Kaden pulled the blanket from his shoulder and stared at him with his all-too-knowing gaze. He had to have heard the gunfire and knew there was something Chris didn't want them to see. He looked at his sister and pulled the blanket over their heads, resting his on Chris's shoulder.

For the first time in hours, Chris took a worry-free breath. His eyes stung and he dropped his head back blinking. *Thanks for not being a dick, Murphy.*

DENISE RUSHED through the automatic Emergency Department

sliding doors, turning sideways to squeeze through before they were wide enough for her.

"Ma'am, unless that dog is a service animal it can't be in here." A guard stepped in front of her, a hand outstretched.

She skidded to a stop. "What?" She looked down at Sprocket and realized she'd forgotten her vest and lead in her car.

"Shit." She looked back at the guard. "She is. I swear." She held out her keys. "Look, here're my keys. Her vest is in the passenger seat."

The guard held his hands up. "Ma'am—"

"Please. My niece and nephew were brought in." She didn't have time to go back for the vest. Sprocket lay down and rested her hands on her paws.

"Denise."

She whipped around and strode to meet Chris.

He flashed his badge at the guard. "I'll escort her back."

The guard nodded and backed away from them.

Chris took her arm and led her through reception and a set of double doors.

"How are they?" she asked.

"They're fine. They're still a little nervous. Kaden bit an orderly when they tried to separate him and Kimber, so I convinced the nurses to examine them in the same room."

"But they're okay? Physically?"

"I promise, Denise. They're fine."

Relief sucker-punched her and her knees buckled. She clutched his arms and he pulled her into his embrace, tucking her head into his neck as tears poured down her face.

"I've got you."

For the first time in longer than she could remember, she didn't hold it in. Didn't lock it down and hide it. The hurt, the pain, the fear. It flowed out of her. She couldn't have stopped it, even if she wanted to. For once, she could not be the strong one.

She needed someone to take the weight from her shoulders and she let Chris do it.

He surrounded her and held her tight. One arm wrapped tightly around her, the palm of his hand cradling the back of her head. His lips warm and firm at her temple and he repeated, "They're okay."

Finally, she nodded and pulled back enough to wipe her palms under her eyes.

"Does she always do that?" Chris asked.

Denise looked up at him, but he was looking down. She followed his gaze and found Sprocket wedged between their legs, lying on their feet. She hadn't even noticed.

A small laugh escaped and she wiped under her nose with the sleeve of her sweatshirt. "Yeah. When I'm not doing okay, she sits on my feet."

"There is one thing." He took a deep breath. "Eddie is dead. He pulled a gun and was shot twice."

Another wave of relief washed through her and she dropped her forehead to his chest. That respite was followed quickly by shame at being glad for the death of another person, no matter how horrible they were, and sorrow for Kaden and Kimber. They'd lost both their parents. Not that Eddie was ever much of a parent, but her heart still broke for them.

She snapped her head up. "Did you...?"

He shook his head. "It wasn't me."

It shouldn't matter. For fuck's sake, she'd tortured a guy for information, but she was glad Chris hadn't been the one to kill Eddie.

"What about your situation?" he asked.

"I called in a favor from an old Army buddy."

"Will you tell me?" His crystal blue eyes gazed into hers with worry.

"Not today."

"Okay." He kissed her forehead. "You ready to see them?"

She nodded.

Chris threaded his fingers through hers and led her a few more doors down the hall to a room with another guard in front.

"Why is there a guard in front of their room?"

"Just to keep non-essential people out, that's all."

Sliding the glass door open, then the curtains, he revealed Kaden and Kimber curled up asleep on the hospital bed.

She let go of Chris's hand and hugged them, pressing kisses to their cheeks and foreheads.

Kimber's eyes fluttered open. "Aunt Denny!" She popped up to her knees and threw herself at Denise, curling her arms and legs around her.

Denise stumbled back a step and felt Chris's hand on her lower back. Catching her balance, she braced her arms under Kimber's butt and turned, sitting on the edge of the bed. Kaden wrapped his arms around her neck. She untangled one arm and hugged him closer.

Looking between their heads, she mouthed, "Thank you," to Chris.

"When can we go home?" Kimber asked.

"Soon. As soon as I talk to the doctor."

"But there's nothing wrong with us," Kaden said.

She brushed his hair back from his face. "I know, but they want to be careful. It won't be long." She looked at Chris for confirmation.

He nodded, then pulled his phone out of his pocket. Holding up a finger, he stepped out of the room, putting the phone to his ear.

Kaden's arms had a strangle hold on her and he mumbled something into her shoulder.

"What, buddy?"

"I'm sorry." His small shoulders shook.

"Hey. What are you sorry for?"

"Weshouldn'thavegonewithhimbutheknewourcodeword."

She tried to lean away to hear him better. "What?"

It came out in a rush of words again and it took a moment for it to click. Eddie had known what their code word was. That was how he'd gotten them out of the school so easily. Why the secretary said she hadn't sensed any problem when the police had questioned her.

There was no undoing the past, but she'd be damned if he blamed himself for what happened.

"Kaden, look at me." She shrugged her shoulder to get him to pick up his head.

He lifted tear-swollen eyes to hers.

"This is not your fault."

"But I knew something wasn't right. Even though he knew our word. I didn't think about it until later that *you* didn't know what our word was so no one should have known what it was."

"I want you to listen to me very carefully. This is *not* your fault. If it hadn't happened today, it would have happened some other day and maybe someone would have gotten hurt." She flinched a little on the inside because someone had been hurt, but not because of anything Kaden had done. "You kept you and your sister safe. That is what's important. Okay?"

He nodded, but she didn't think he believed her. The guilt was going to stay with him for a long time, but she'd help him understand that there was no second-guessing the past. She pulled his head down and kissed his temple.

"What is your code word?"

"Pipsqueak," he said.

She squeezed her eyes closed as the tears started again. That had been her nickname for Sarah for as long as she could remember. She'd hated it.

"How could he know?" Kaden asked.

At one time, Sarah had loved Eddie. She'd been excited to start a family and probably talked about all kinds of things with the man she thought was going to be their father. Including how to keep them safe from people like him. She couldn't even begin to explain all that to them.

"I don't know. Maybe your mom told him that I called her that when we were little and he guessed."

"I want to go home," Kimber said.

"I know, baby." Denise kissed her forehead. "I want to go home, too. Soon, okay?"

She laid her head down on Denise's shoulder. "Okay."

Denise felt the rise and fall of her back under her hand and squeezed her eyes closed, quietly blowing out a breath. Kaden rested against her shoulder and she dropped her head on top of his.

Chris opened the door and beckoned for her to come out.

"Let me talk to Chris real quick and then I'll find the doctor so we can leave, okay?"

"Okay," Kaden said.

She patted Kimber's back and helped her slide off her lap onto the bed. Stepping from the room, she pulled the door closed behind her. "Is everything okay?"

He looked down at his phone, then at her through his lashes. "I need to go."

"Okay," she said.

"I'll try to be in touch."

Wait. He—What? Her stomach flipped. He was leaving, leaving. She closed her eyes and swallowed hard. She wanted to ask him to stay. To choose her over his job, but she couldn't. It was important to him, so she did what she did best. She sucked it up, locked it down, and pretended to be strong.

She opened her eyes. "Okay."

He stared at her, opened his mouth and closed it again, then said, "Okay." He turned and walked away.

She took a bracing breath before going back into the room. A hand on her arm spun her around and he grasped her face and kissed her. His tongue delved deep as he pulled her close. She went up on her toes and inhaled sharply through her nose. She wanted it to go on forever and it ended too soon.

He released her and stared at her for several heartbeats. "I love you." Then he left.

She gaped after his retreating back. Turning in a half-circle, she looked at the guard trying his best not to smile or look directly at her. She threw up her hands. "What the hell am I supposed to do with that?"

CHAPTER 26

*D*enise checked the caller ID on the phone before answering. Only a few people had the number at the cabin, but they still got random calls from solicitors. She smiled when she saw the name.

"Hey. How're you?"

"Funny," Bree said. "That's the same question I was going to ask you. I feel like I haven't talked to you in forever."

She walked across the kitchen to the sliding glass doors and out to the raised back deck. "I know. I'm sorry. I haven't really felt up to making the effort."

"Do you want me to let you go?"

"No!" Hearing Bree's voice, she realized how much she missed her. "I want to talk to you. I just…I didn't realize I needed to until I heard your voice."

"I get it. How are the kids?"

She stared down at the dock where her parents had taken them after breakfast. Their shrieks of laughter echoed off the lake as they jumped off the dock and swam. Sweetpea loved the water as much as Kaden and Kimber and jumped right along with them.

"They're good. Getting them into therapy right away helped,

215

but it's going to take a while before they're a hundred percent." She sighed and leaned against the wood railing.

"How're things going at the rescue?" she asked. A tiny kernel of guilt lodged in her stomach, but she shoved it back down. She loved the rescue, but taking care of Kaden and Kimber was more important.

"The new office manager is working out really well. She asked if she could use the changes she's making for her process improvement project for one of her management classes. I told her to go for it. I hope that's okay?"

"Of course it is. What does a good grade mean? We absolutely sucked and she had to redo everything or she only had to make minor improvements for efficiency?"

Bree laughed. "No idea. Which do you want it to be?"

"Hopefully I didn't screw it up that bad."

"You've managed to bring in a profit the last few years, so I doubt it."

"How are you and Jase settling in together?"

"We're good."

"You hesitated. Why did you hesitate?" Christ, if this shit screwed them up on top of everything else, she might very well lose her shit again.

"Normal learning to live together stuff. The man leaves his socks everywhere. And not both socks. One sock of a pair. Actually not even a pair, since I don't think he has a matching pair."

Tension in her shoulders released. Bree ranting meant Bree was annoyed, not ready to stab someone. Bree ranting was a good thing.

She listened half-heartedly and picked at the chipped stain on the railing.

"Have you heard from Chris at all?" Bree asked.

She quit picking at the chips. "A couple of texts from random numbers, but when I tried to call them back they're not in service."

"What did they say?"

"The first one said *miss you* and the second one said *be home soon*."

"When was the last one?"

"A week or so, I guess?"

"Have you tried to call since then?"

Too many times to count. "Not in a couple of days."

"You okay?" Bree asked.

"Yeah. I'm just…you know. Doing that girly thing I hate doing."

"Pining?"

"That's such a stupid word. I'm questioning and second-guessing." Was he coming back? Would it be the same now that he didn't have a reason to be with her? Did he really mean to tell her he loved her? Why didn't he give her a chance to say it back?

"So…pining."

"Moist."

"That doesn't bother me."

"Irregardless."

Bree gasped. "You didn't."

"I did. I've got more where that came from."

"Fine! I won't say you're…you know…anymore."

"Thank you."

"You know what your problem is?"

Denise rolled her eyes and dropped her head to her forearm where it rested on the railing. "If I say yes, can I avoid this next part?"

"No. You're a closet romantic."

"Do what now?"

"Face it. You *say* you hate all the girly stuff, but secretly you want Chris to come riding in on a white horse and sweep you off your feet."

"I'm gonna have to go with no."

"I'm bringing all my Disney movies up with me and we're going to watch all of them until you admit it."

She smiled in spite of the Disney threat. "I've missed you."

"Aw. I've missed you, too. We're still planning on being there for Labor Day weekend. That was actually the reason I called—to make sure it was still okay for us to come up."

"Of course it is. Kaden and Kimber are excited to see you. Gran won't come?"

"And I quote, 'If God wanted me to be in the wilderness he wouldn't have made cities.'"

"She does know this house has four bedrooms, right?" It even had satellite since her mom refused to rough it any more than Bree's grandmother.

"She thinks it's a log cabin with a moss roof. Hey. I've got to go. I sent you a present, so don't shoot anyone coming up the drive."

"What present?"

"It's a surprise, silly. I'll see you in a few days. Love you."

"Love you, too."

She disconnected the line and stared down at the phone, then dialed Chris's number. Expecting it to go straight to voicemail, she stood upright when it rang more than once. Shit! She didn't know what she was going to say. She'd dialed out of habit—she hadn't believed it would actually ring.

Her heart pounded in her chest and sweat formed under her arms.

"Hey."

"Hi. I—"

"I can't answer the phone. Leave a message."

Her shoulders sagged and she tried to look on the positive side. At least it was ringing now.

"Hey. It's me. Denise. I keep trying your number and this is the first time it didn't go straight to voicemail. I didn't leave any messages before since I didn't know if you'd get them. I'm not even sure why I tried calling this time, but I... We're up at my parents' cabin and the cell reception is bad and I didn't know if you were trying to call or… Anyway. Um. I'll talk to you later."

She ended the call and banged her head against the railing. She. Was. Such. A. Spaz.

Ugh.

Lifting her head, she watched her mom wrap a towel around Kimber, then pull her into her lap. She was grateful her parents had been able to spend a few weeks with her and the kids. Kaden and Kimber had needed them as much as she had. There was just something about having your mom and dad with you when you felt like shit.

Tears pricked the backs of her eyes. Rubbing them with the heels of her hands, she tried to shove them back in. Something else she'd been doing a lot of lately. Doc Tailor had told her it was years of suppressed emotion finally having a way out.

By her own estimation she should be done crying sometime in the next ten to twelve years.

Sprocket whined and leaned against her leg. She reached down and rubbed behind one of her ears. Her dog had barely left her side in the last few months. She'd tried to dig a hole in the bathroom door one morning when Denise had accidentally shut her out.

"Aunt Denny," Kaden yelled from the path below.

She rubbed at her eyes a final time and looked down. Kaden ran ahead of her parents, who were holding Kimber's hands. Sweetpea foraged along the side of the path.

She waved at Kaden. "Hey, buddy. Hungry?"

"Yes! Grandpa said I could help make hamburgers for lunch."

"Cool," she said. "After you take a shower."

"Aunt Denny," Kaden whined. "We were in the lake."

"I know," she said. "And now you're covered in fish pee. You need to wash that stuff off before you stick your hands in my food."

"Fish pee? Argh!" Kaden ran the rest of the way up the path and she heard the door downstairs open and slam.

Kimber stayed next to her grandmother, either unconcerned about being covered in fish pee or she recognized the *Moana* reference since she and Bree had watched it on a loop for an entire weekend.

She was envious of their resiliency. They still had the occasional nightmares and Kaden had his heart set on taking karate lessons so he could fight the bad guys, but for the most part they'd bounced back surprisingly well. Being surrounded by love and support helped tremendously—something she constantly reminded herself of.

Going back into the house, she set the phone on the cradle on her way to the kitchen. Everyone came up the stairs from the basement at the same time.

"Sweetie, someone was coming up the drive as we were walking up," her mom said. "Can you see who it is while we shower and change? I'll give Kimber a quick bath."

"Sure. Bree said she'd sent me a present, so it's probably the delivery guy."

"That's sweet of her. Aren't they coming up for the long weekend? Why couldn't she have brought it then?"

Denise shrugged. "Dunno. She didn't say."

"Well, hopefully it's something worth the delivery fee. Can't imagine it didn't cost her an arm and a leg to have something sent all the way out here."

Her dad was looking at her mom like she'd lost her mind.

"What?" her mom asked. "They'll be here in a week. They could have saved the money and brought it with them. I'm only saying." She threw her hands up in the air and turned toward the bedrooms. "Far be it from me to suggest anyone be fiscally responsible."

Shaking his head, her father said, "I'll be quick."

"Okay." She crossed the house to the front door and opened it as a large black, extended-cab pickup truck crested the small hill in front of the house.

Her breath caught in her throat and her heart danced a few fast beats before settling back into a steady, thumping rhythm.

His hair was long again. He rounded the front of the truck and walked toward her, concern pinching the center of his brows together.

He climbed halfway up the steps and stopped when they were eye level. "Why are you crying?"

Was she? She hadn't realized. Shaking her head, she said, "Water main break. I can't stop it."

He shoved his hands in his pockets. "I'd hoped you'd be happy to see me."

The uncertainty in his voice killed her. "I am. I am so fucking happy to see you."

"I'd feel better about this whole thing if you could stop crying."

"Doc said I'm overdue, so it may be a while before that happens."

He climbed one more step, forcing her to tilt her head back. "What can I do to help?"

"Touch me."

His hands clasped the sides of her face and he touched his lips to hers. Throwing her arms around his neck, she pressed her body as close as she could with one step still between them. She wanted to wrap herself around him. Put her hands on every inch of him. Have his weight press down on her.

The screen door slammed and a throat cleared. "Son. I'm going to have to ask you what your intentions are toward my daughter."

Trust her dad to kill the moment. That must have been why he'd looked at her mom like she was crazy. He'd known Chris was coming. She didn't know whether to punch him or hug him. Maybe both.

Chris broke their kiss and stared at her. "Well, sir, I plan on declaring my undying love and devotion to your daughter."

"Jesus. You couldn't have found someone normal?"

The screen door slammed again, so she assumed her dad went back inside and the question was rhetorical.

"Is normal what you want?" Chris asked.

"I think normal would be pretty damn boring."

He brushed the hair away from her face. "Me, too."

"What does declaring your undying love and devotion mean, exactly?"

"For starters, it means one day he's going to ask me that question and I'm going to ask his permission to marry you."

For once in her life she didn't have a snappy comeback. She must look like a fish because all she could do was open and close her mouth.

"In the meantime, it means I'm not leaving you again."

She shook her head. "You can't make those kinds of promises, Chris. With your job—"

"I quit."

"You—What?" He'd knocked her speechless for the second time in only moments.

"They wanted to transfer me to Arizona. I said no. I'm not leaving you again. That's one of the reasons it took me so long to get up here. I had to process out of the Bureau."

"You can't do that for me." She tried to lower her arms, but he held her tighter.

"I did it for us. I also did it just for me. I was burning out, Denise. Fast. I knew I needed to make a change, but I didn't know what to do. Jase offered me a partnership in V.E.T. Adventures. I accepted."

"Oh." He'd quit. For her. For them, but also for her. She licked her lips. "Does it mean anything else?"

His thumb brushed across her bottom lip. "Yeah, it does. It means I'm in love with you and I plan on being in love with you for a very long time."

"Oh." The tears stopped. Everything stopped. The doubt and

fear. Everything inside her fell into place as if it been a swirling mass that finally settled into calm, peaceful bliss.

"Oh. I can wait until you're ready to say it, too."

She shook her head. "Today."

"You're going to say it today?"

"No. Yes." She wasn't making any sense. "I love you. Marry me. Today."

He blinked at her. "Today, today?"

"Yes. Gatlinburg is three hours from here. There're wedding chapels all over the place. It's not Vegas, but I'm sure we can find something."

A blinding grin spread across his face. "You're serious."

"Fuck yes, I'm serious." She had never been more serious about anything in her life than she was of the man standing in front of her. "I don't want a big wedding. Almost everyone I want to invite is here. Bree might kill me, but she'll get over it." She shrugged. "In a couple of years."

He kissed her deeply and possessively. She was consumed and rebuilt. Weakened and strengthened. He took everything she had and gave her everything she'd ever need.

"Do I still need to ask your dad for permission?"

The screen door opened and Kaden tromped out followed by a bouncing Kimber and her mom. "Come on, kids, everyone in the car."

"We want to ride with Chris and Aunt Denny," Kimber said.

Denise raised her eyebrows at Chris.

"Sure, they can ride with us."

"Yay!" Kimber skipped to the truck and waited for her grandmother to open the door.

Her dad came out of the house and pulled the door shut behind him. He held a ring out to Chris. "You're going to need this. It was Karen's mother's." He kissed Denise on the temple and strode down the steps to help her mom with the kids.

They both stared down at the ring. "I guess this means I have his permission."

Denise grinned. "I guess so."

He stepped up onto the porch, then knelt down on one knee. "Denise. Will you marry me?"

She threw her head back and laughed, then held her left hand out. "Yes. I will marry you."

Chris stood and wiped the back of his hand across his forehead. "Whew. Thank goodness. That was one of the most nerve-racking things I've ever done." He slid the ring over her finger. "Can't tell you how long I practiced that speech."

The ring wouldn't go past her knuckle.

"Uh oh," he said. "Is this a bad omen?"

Pulling the ring off, she rolled her eyes. "It means my grandmother was all of five-foot-two and ninety-pounds with all her clothes on. We'll get it sized."

He stopped her from stepping off the porch. "Denise. Are you sure this is what you want?"

She could see the concern in his eyes. "I want you. I want a life with you. There's no amount of planning or waiting or tulle that's going to change that."

His arms banded around her so tightly it squeezed the breath right out of her. Or maybe it was the overwhelming happiness that made her breathless.

"I love you," he whispered.

She smiled. "I love you."

"Aunt Denny," Kimber called, hanging out the window. "Grandpa wants to know if we're going anytime soon and if you're going to stay here and make decorations all day."

"Decorations?" Chris asked.

"Declarations," she explained.

"Ah. I can make my declarations on the drive just as well as I can make them here. Oh! Wait. One more thing." He reached into his back pocket and pulled out a small envelope. "I came with a card."

She took it and ripped along the seam to open the envelope. "So you're my present?"

"I was going to wear nothing but a bow, but with your parents and the kids, I thought it might be a little much."

Flipping open the simple card with a heart on the cover, she threw her head back and laughed.

"What's so funny?" he asked.

She handed him the card. "Remind me we need to take a selfie with that showing off our rings."

And they all lived happily ever after. The End. Team Chris for the win! :P

"She's going to be so mad at you."

"But you love me, right?"

"Damn skippy."

AFTERWORD

I think it bears repeating that this is a work of fiction. I took *extreme* artistic license with parts of Denise's storyline. It is true that atrocities were committed by a small, outlier group of people in Iraq. They did not, in any way, represent the vast majority of service members who served and fought with honor and distinction.

***

There are many, many animal rescues throughout the United States. Several of them work to rehabilitate dogs and train them to be service animals for veterans and people with disabilities. I encourage you to find one in your local area and donate, volunteer, and follow them on social media. And *please*, if you're thinking about adding a fur baby to your family... Adopt. Don't shop.

ACKNOWLEDGMENTS

I find the acknowledgements to be the hardest part of finishing a book. Weird, huh? But how do I express my gratitude to everyone who helps make this goal a reality without sounding trite? But…here goes:

El. Even though I dedicated it to you, thank you for being my person. Iraq was hell and I'm pretty sure the only reason I made it through was because of you.

Toni. My RT platonic romance. My line standing partner. My travel buddy. Thank you for your friendship, your humor, and your strength.

Taylor at Imagination Uncovered. Thank you SO much for another gorgeous cover!

Shauna Kruse, Matthew Hosea, and Stephanie Pietz for such a gorgeous photo.

Jessica Snyder, editor extraordinaire. Do what you're told! I don't care if I'm not your real mom! lol. Thank you so much for your guidance and direction and superb attention to detail. Peen-to: any of several peaches with a flattened shape; *especially* :a peach of Chinese origin grown in the southern U.S.

The A2T2 Reader Group. You're the best group of readers because you're mine! Well, one-fourth mine, but you get my point.

The reviewers, bloggers, sharers: Thank you for your support, your likes, and your shares.

The readers: *Thank you. Thank you. Thank you.* You're the reason I keep doing this. Also because the voices in my head tell me to, but mostly because of you.

ABOUT THE AUTHOR

Tarina has spent her entire life in and around the military - first as a dependent and then as an enlisted Air Force member.

In 2015, a friend challenged her to complete NaNoWriMo. She dusted off one of the many stories she'd started over the years, threw it in the trash, and started all over.

Her debut novel, Stitched Up Heart, released in September 2016. The military gives her plenty of material to work with and she strives to create characters who authentically represent all facets of the military life - the good and the not so great.

Tarina is still active duty, a single mom of five-year-old twins, and a closet romantic. Her favorite hobby is sleep. She has delusions of retiring from the military and being a stay-at-home mom.

Sign up for her newsletter, join the A2T2 Reader Group, and follow her on Bookbub and Instagram.

www.tarinadeaton.com
tarinadeaton@gmail.com

ALSO BY TARINA DEATON

Stitched Up Heart

Rescued Heart

Half-Broke Heart